The KINGS TREASURIES
OF LITERATURE

GENERAL EDITOR
SIR A·T· QUILLER COUCH

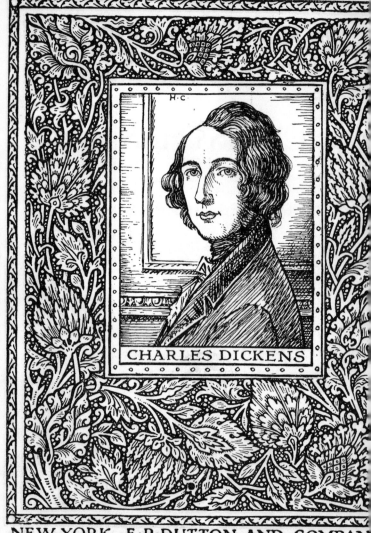

CHARLES DICKENS

NEW YORK E·P·DUTTON AND COMPAN

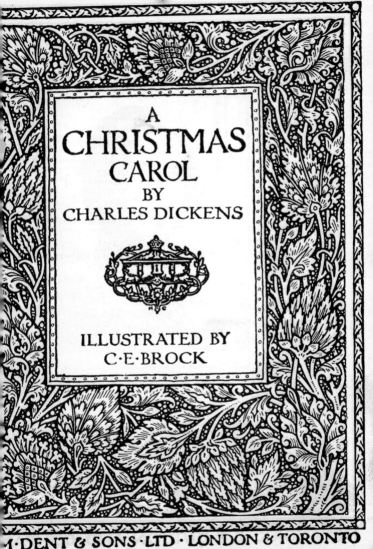

A CHRISTMAS CAROL

BY
CHARLES DICKENS

ILLUSTRATED BY
C·E·BROCK

J·M·DENT & SONS·LTD·LONDON & TORONTO

First Published in this Edition . 1921
Reprinted 1922, 1925, 1926, 1928,
1930

PRINTED IN GREAT BRITAIN

CONTENTS

LIST OF ILLUSTRATIONS

I have endeavoured in this Ghostly little book, to raise the Ghost of an Idea, which shall not put my readers out of humour with themselves, with each other, with the season, or with me. May it haunt their houses pleasantly, and no one wish to lay it.

Their faithful friend and Servant,

C. D.

December, 1843.

A Christmas Carol
Stave One
Marley's Ghost

*No beggars implored
him to bestow a trifle*

MARLEY was dead: to begin with. There is no doubt whatever about that. The register of his burial was signed by the clergyman, the clerk, the undertaker, and the chief mourner. Scrooge signed it: and Scrooge's name was good upon 'Change, for anything he chose to put his hand to. Old Marley was as dead as a door-nail.

Mind! I don't mean to say that I know, of my own knowledge, what there is particularly dead about a door-nail. I might have been inclined, myself, to regard a coffin-nail as the deadest piece of ironmongery in the trade. But the wisdom of our ancestors is in the simile; and my unhallowed hands shall not disturb it, or the Country's done for. You will therefore permit me to repeat, emphatically, that Marley was as dead as a door-nail.

Scrooge knew he was dead? Of course he did. How could it be otherwise? Scrooge and he were partners for I don't know how many years. Scrooge was his sole executor, his sole administrator, his sole assign, his sole residuary legatee, his sole friend and sole mourner. And even Scrooge was not so dreadfully cut up by the sad event, but that he was an excellent man of business on the day of the funeral, and solemnised it with an undoubted bargain.

The mention of Marley's funeral brings me back to the point I started from. There is no doubt that Marley was dead. This must be distinctly understood, or nothing wonderful can come of the story I am going to relate. If we were not perfectly convinced that Hamlet's Father died before the play began, there would be nothing more remarkable in his taking a stroll at night, in an easterly wind, upon his own ramparts, than there would be in any other middle-aged gentleman rashly turning out after dark in a breezy spot—say St. Paul's Churchyard, for instance—literally to astonish his son's weak mind.

Scrooge never painted out old Marley's name. There it stood, years afterwards, above the warehouse door: Scrooge and Marley. The firm was known as Scrooge and Marley. Sometimes people new to the business called Scrooge Scrooge, and sometimes Marley, but he answered to both names: it was all the same to him.

Oh! But he was a tight-fisted hand at the grindstone, Scrooge! a squeezing, wrenching, grasping, scraping, clutching, covetous, old sinner! Hard and sharp as flint, from which no steel had ever struck out generous fire; secret, and self-contained, and solitary as an oyster. The cold within him froze his old features, nipped his pointed nose, shrivelled his cheek, stiffened his gait; made his eyes red, his thin lips blue; and spoke out shrewdly in his grating voice. A frosty rime was on his head, and on his eyebrows, and his wiry chin. He carried his own low temperature always about with him; he iced his office in the dog-days; and didn't thaw it one degree at Christmas.

External heat and cold had little influence on Scrooge. No warmth could warm, nor wintry

weather chill him. No wind that blew was bitterer
than he, no falling snow was more intent upon its
purpose, no pelting rain less open to entreaty.
Foul weather didn't know where to have him.
The heaviest rain, and snow, and hail, and sleet,
could boast of the advantage over him in only
one respect. They often "came down" handsomely, and Scrooge never did.

Nobody ever stopped him in the street to say,
with gladsome looks, "My dear Scrooge, how
are you? When will you come to see me?" No
beggars implored him to bestow a trifle, no children asked him what it was o'clock, no man or
woman ever once in all his life inquired the way
to such and such a place, of Scrooge. Even the
blind men's dogs appeared to know him; and
when they saw him coming on, would tug their
owners into doorways and up courts; and then
would wag their tails as though they said,
"No eye at all is better than an evil eye, dark
master!"

But what did Scrooge care? It was the very
thing he liked. To edge his way along the crowded
paths of life, warning all human sympathy to
keep its distance, was what the knowing ones
call "nuts" to Scrooge.

Once upon a time—of all the good days in
the year, on Christmas Eve—old Scrooge sat

busy in his counting-house. It was cold, bleak, biting weather: foggy withal: and he could hear the people in the court outside go wheezing up and down, beating their hands upon their breasts, and stamping their feet upon the pavement-stones to warm them. The City clocks had only just gone three, but it was quite dark already: it had not been light all day: and candles were flaring in the windows of the neighbouring offices, like ruddy smears upon the palpable brown air. The fog came pouring in at every chink and key-hole, and was so dense without, that although the court was of the narrowest, the houses opposite were mere phantoms. To see the dingy cloud come drooping down, obscuring everything, one might have thought that Nature lived hard by, and was brewing on a large scale.

The door of Scrooge's counting-house was open that he might keep his eye upon his clerk, who in a dismal little cell beyond, a sort of tank, was copying letters. Scrooge had a very small fire, but the clerk's fire was so very much smaller that it looked like one coal. But he couldn't replenish it, for Scrooge kept the coal-box in his own room; and so surely as the clerk came in with the shovel, the master predicted that it would be necessary for them to part. Wherefore the clerk put on his white comforter, and tried to warm himself

C.E.Brock
1905

at the candle; in which effort, not being a man of a strong imagination, he failed.

"A merry Christmas, uncle! God save you!" cried a cheerful voice. It was the voice of Scrooge's nephew, who came upon him so quickly that this was the first intimation he had of his approach.

"Bah!" said Scrooge, "Humbug!"

He had so heated himself with rapid walking in the fog and frost, this nephew of Scrooge's, that he was all in a glow; his face was ruddy and handsome; his eyes sparkled, and his breath smoked again.

"Christmas a humbug, uncle!" said Scrooge's nephew. "You don't mean that, I am sure."

"I do," said Scrooge. "Merry Christmas! What right have you to be merry? What reason have you to be merry? You're poor enough."

"Come, then," returned the nephew, gaily. "What right have you to be dismal? What reason have you to be morose? You're rich enough."

Scrooge having no better answer ready on the spur of the moment, said, "Bah!" again: and followed it up with "Humbug."

"Don't be cross, uncle," said the nephew.

"What else can I be," returned the uncle, "when I live in such a world of fools as this? Merry Christmas! Out upon merry Christmas! What's Christmas time to you but a time for paying bills without money; a time for finding yourself a year older, but not an hour richer; a time for balancing your books and having every item in 'em through a round dozen of months presented dead against you? If I could work my will," said Scrooge, indignantly, "every idiot who goes about with 'Merry Christmas' on his lips, should be boiled with his own pudding, and buried with a stake of holly through his heart. He should!"

"Uncle!" pleaded the nephew.

"Nephew!" returned the uncle, sternly, "keep Christmas in your own way, and let me keep it in mine."

"Keep it!" repeated Scrooge's nephew. "But you don't keep it."

"Let me leave it alone, then," said Scrooge. "Much good may it do you! Much good it has ever done you!"

"There are many things from which I might have derived good, by which I have not profited, I dare say," returned the nephew: "Christmas among the rest. But I am sure I have always thought of Christmas time, when it has come round — apart from the veneration due to its sacred name and origin, if anything belonging to it can be apart from that—as a good time: a kind, forgiving, charitable, pleasant time: the only time I know of, in the long calendar of the year, when men and women seem by one consent to open their shut-up hearts freely, and to think of people below them as if they really were fellow-passengers to the grave, and not another race of creatures bound on other journeys. And therefore, uncle, though it has never put a scrap of gold or silver in my pocket, I believe that it *has* done me good, and *will* do me good; and I say, God bless it!"

The clerk in the Tank involuntarily applauded: becoming immediately sensible of the impropriety, he poked the fire, and extinguished the last frail spark for ever.

"Let me hear another sound from *you*," said Scrooge, "and you'll keep your Christmas by losing your situation. You're quite a powerful speaker, sir," he added, turning to his nephew. "I wonder you don't go into Parliament."

"Don't be angry, uncle. Come! Dine with us to-morrow."

Scrooge said that he would see him—yes, indeed he did. He went the whole length of the expression, and said that he would see him in that extremity first.

"But why?" cried Scrooge's nephew. "Why?"

"Why did you get married?" said Scrooge.

"Because I fell in love."

"Because you fell in love!" growled Scrooge, as if that were the only one thing in the world more ridiculous than a merry Christmas. "Good afternoon!"

"Nay, uncle, but you never came to see me before that happened. Why give it as a reason for not coming now?"

"Good afternoon!" said Scrooge.

" I want nothing from you; I ask nothing of you; why cannot we be friends? "

" Good afternoon! " said Scrooge.

" I am sorry, with all my heart, to find you so resolute. We have never had any quarrel, to which I have been a party. But I have made the trial in homage to Christmas, and I'll keep my Christmas humour to the last. So A Merry Christmas, uncle! "

" Good afternoon! " said Scrooge.

" And a Happy New Year! "

" Good afternoon! " said Scrooge.

His nephew left the room without an angry word, notwithstanding. He stopped at the outer door to bestow the greetings of the season on the clerk, who, cold as he was, was warmer than Scrooge; for he returned them cordially.

" There's another fellow," muttered Scrooge, who overheard him: " my clerk, with fifteen shillings a-week, and a wife and family, talking about a merry Christmas. I'll retire to Bedlam."

This lunatic, in letting Scrooge's nephew out, had let two other people in. They were portly gentlemen, pleasant to behold, and now stood, with their hats off, in Scrooge's office. They had books and papers in their hands, and bowed to him.

" Scrooge and Marley's, I believe," said one

of the gentlemen, referring to his list. " Have I the pleasure of addressing Mr. Scrooge, or Mr. Marley? "

" Mr. Marley has been dead these seven years," Scrooge replied. " He died seven years ago, this very night."

" We have no doubt his liberality is well represented by his surviving partner," said the gentleman, presenting his credentials.

It certainly was; for they had been two kindred spirits. At the ominous word " liberality," Scrooge frowned, and shook his head, and handed the credentials back.

" At this festive season of the year, Mr. Scrooge," said the gentleman, taking up a pen, " it is more than usually desirable that we should make some slight provision for the poor and destitute, who suffer greatly at the present time. Many thousands are in want of common necessaries; hundreds of thousands are in want of common comforts, sir."

" Are there no prisons? " asked Scrooge.

" Plenty of prisons," said the gentleman, laying down the pen again.

" And the Union workhouses? " demanded Scrooge. " Are they still in operation? "

" They are. Still," returned the gentleman, " I wish I could say they were not."

"The Treadmill and the Poor Law are in full vigour, then?" said Scrooge.

"Both very busy, sir."

"Oh! I was afraid, from what you said at first, that something had occurred to stop them in their useful course," said Scrooge. "I'm very glad to hear it."

"Under the impression that they scarcely furnish Christian cheer of mind or body to the multitude," returned the gentleman, "a few of us are endeavouring to raise a fund to buy the Poor some meat and drink, and means of warmth. We choose this time, because it is a time, of all others, when Want is keenly felt, and Abundance rejoices. What shall I put you down for?"

"Nothing!" Scrooge replied.

"You wish to be anonymous?"

"I wish to be left alone," said Scrooge. "Since you ask me what I wish, gentlemen, that is my answer. I don't make merry myself at Christmas, and I can't afford to make idle people merry. I help to support the establishments I have mentioned: they cost enough: and those who are badly off must go there."

"Many can't go there; and many would rather die."

"If they would rather die," said Scrooge, "they had better do it, and decrease the surplus population. Besides—excuse me—I don't know that."

"But you might know it," observed the gentleman.

"It's not my business," Scrooge returned. "It's enough for a man to understand his own business, and not to interfere with other people's. Mine occupies me constantly. Good afternoon, gentlemen!"

Seeing clearly that it would be useless to pursue their point, the gentlemen withdrew. Scrooge resumed his labours with an improved opinion of himself, and in a more facetious temper than was usual with him.

Meanwhile the fog and darkness thickened so, that people ran about with flaring links, proffering their services to go before horses in carriages, and conduct them on their way. The ancient tower of a church, whose gruff old bell was always peeping slily down at Scrooge out of a Gothic window in the wall, became invisible, and struck the hours and quarters in the clouds, with tremulous vibrations afterwards as if its teeth were chattering in its frozen head up there. The cold became intense. In the main street at the corner of the court, some labourers were repairing the gas-pipes, and had lighted a great fire in a brazier, round which a party of ragged men and boys

were gathered: warming their hands and winking their eyes before the blaze in rapture. The
water-plug being left in solitude, its overflowings
sullenly congealed, and turned to misanthropic
ice. The brightness of the shops where holly
sprigs and berries crackled in the lamp heat of
the windows, made pale faces ruddy as they
passed. Poulterers' and grocers' trades became
a splendid joke: a glorious pageant, with which
it was next to impossible to believe that such
dull principles as bargain and sale had anything
to do. The Lord Mayor, in the stronghold of
the mighty Mansion House, gave orders to his
fifty cooks and butlers to keep Christmas as a
Lord Mayor's household should; and even the
little tailor, whom he had fined five shillings on
the previous Monday for being drunk and blood-
thirsty in the streets, stirred up to-morrow's
pudding in his garret, while his lean wife and the
baby sallied out to buy the beef.

Foggier yet, and colder! Piercing, searching,
biting cold. If the good Saint Dunstan had but
nipped the Evil Spirit's nose with a touch of such
weather as that, instead of using his familiar
weapons, then indeed he would have roared to
lusty purpose. The owner of one scant young
nose, gnawed and mumbled by the hungry cold
as bones are gnawed by dogs, stooped down at

Scrooge's keyhole to regale him with a Christmas Carol: but at the first sound of

> God bless you, merry gentleman!
> May nothing you dismay!

Scrooge seized the ruler with such energy of action, that the singer fled in terror, leaving the keyhole to the fog and even more congenial frost.

At length the hour of shutting up the counting-house arrived. With an ill-will Scrooge dismounted from his stool, and tacitly admitted the fact to the expectant clerk in the Tank, who instantly snuffed his candle out, and put on his hat.

" You'll want all day to-morrow, I suppose? " said Scrooge.

" If quite convenient, sir."

" It's not convenient," said Scrooge, " and it's not fair. If I was to stop half-a-crown for it, you'd think yourself ill-used, I'll be bound? "

The clerk smiled faintly.

" And yet," said Scrooge, " you don't think *me* ill-used, when I pay a day's wages for no work."

The clerk observed that it was only once a year.

" A poor excuse for picking a man's pocket every twenty-fifth of December! " said Scrooge, buttoning his great-coat to the chin. "But I suppose you must have the whole day. Be here all the earlier next morning!"

The clerk promised that he would; and Scrooge walked out with a growl. The office was closed in a twinkling, and the clerk, with the long ends of his white comforter dangling below his waist (for he boasted no great-coat), went down a slide on Cornhill, at the end of a lane of boys, twenty times, in honour of its being Christmas Eve, and then ran home to Camden Town as hard as he could pelt, to play at blindman's-buff.

Scrooge took his melancholy dinner in his usual melancholy tavern; and having read all the newspapers, and beguiled the rest of the evening with his banker's-book, went home to bed. He lived in chambers which had once belonged to his deceased partner. They were a gloomy suite of rooms, in a lowering pile of building up a yard, where it had so little business to be, that one could scarcely help fancying it must have run there when it was a young house, playing at hide-and-seek with other houses, and have forgotten the way out again. It was old enough now, and dreary enough, for nobody lived in it but Scrooge, the other rooms being all let out as offices. The yard was so dark that even Scrooge, who knew its every stone, was fain to grope with his hands.

The fog and frost so hung about the black old gateway of the house, that it seemed as if the Genius of the Weather sat in mournful meditation on the threshold.

Now, it is a fact, that there was nothing at all particular about the knocker on the door, except that it was very large. It is also a fact, that Scrooge had seen it, night and morning, during his whole residence in that place; also that Scrooge had as little of what is called fancy about him as any man in the City of London, even including—which is a bold word—the corporation, aldermen, and livery. Let it also be borne in mind that Scrooge had not bestowed one thought on Marley, since his last mention of his seven-years' dead partner that afternoon. And then let any man explain to me, if he can, how it happened that Scrooge, having his key in the lock of the door, saw in the knocker, without its undergoing any intermediate process of change: not a knocker, but Marley's face.

Marley's face. It was not in impenetrable shadow as the other objects in the yard were, but had a dismal light about it, like a bad lobster in a dark cellar. It was not angry or ferocious, but looked at Scrooge as Marley used to look: with ghostly spectacles turned up on its ghostly forehead. The hair was curiously stirred, as if

by breath or hot air; and, though the eyes were
wide open, they were perfectly motionless. That,
and its livid colour, made it horrible; but its
horror seemed to be in spite of the face and
beyond its control, rather than a part of its
own expression.

As Scrooge looked fixedly at this phenomenon,
it was a knocker again.

To say that he was not startled, or that his
blood was not conscious of a terrible sensation
to which it had been a stranger from infancy,
would be untrue. But he put his hand upon
the key he had relinquished, turned it sturdily,
walked in, and lighted his candle.

He *did* pause, with a moment's irresolution, before he shut the door; and he *did* look cautiously
behind it first, as if he half-expected to be terrified
with the sight of Marley's pig-tail sticking out
into the hall. But there was nothing on the back
of the door, except the screws and nuts that held
the knocker on; so he said, " Pooh, pooh! " and
closed it with a bang.

The sound resounded through the house like
thunder. Every room above, and every cask
in the wine-merchant's cellars below, appeared
to have a separate peal of echoes of its own.
Scrooge was not a man to be frightened by echoes.
He fastened the door, and walked across the hall,

and up the stairs: slowly too: trimming his candle as he went.

You may talk vaguely about driving a coach-and-six up a good old flight of stairs, or through a bad young Act of Parliament; but I mean to say you might have got a hearse up that stair-case, and taken it broadwise, with the splinter-bar towards the wall, and the door towards the balustrades: and done it easy. There was plenty of width for that, and room to spare; which is perhaps the reason why Scrooge thought he saw a locomotive hearse going on before him in the gloom. Half-a-dozen gas-lamps out of the street wouldn't have lighted the entry too well, so you may suppose that it was pretty dark with Scrooge's dip.

Up Scrooge went, not caring a button for that: darkness is cheap, and Scrooge liked it. But before he shut his heavy door, he walked through his rooms to see that all was right. He had just enough recollection of the face to desire to do that.

Sitting-room, bedroom, lumber-room. All as they should be. Nobody under the table, nobody under the sofa; a small fire in the grate; spoon and basin ready; and the little saucepan of gruel (Scrooge had a cold in his head) upon the hob. Nobody under the bed; nobody in the closet; nobody in his dressing-gown, which was hanging up in a suspicious attitude against the wall. Lumber-room as usual. Old fire-guard, old shoes, two fish-baskets, washing-stand on three legs, and a poker.

Quite satisfied, he closed his door, and locked himself in; double-locked himself in, which was not his custom. Thus secured against surprise, he took off his cravat; put on his dressing-gown and slippers, and his nightcap; and sat down before the fire to take his gruel.

It was a very low fire indeed; nothing on such a bitter night. He was obliged to sit close to it, and brood over it, before he could extract the least sensation of warmth from such a handful of fuel. The fireplace was an old one, built by some Dutch merchant long ago, and paved all round with quaint Dutch tiles, designed to illustrate the Scriptures. There were Cains and Abels, Pharaohs' daughters, Queens of Sheba, Angelic messengers descending through the air on clouds like feather-beds, Abrahams, Belshazzars, Apostles putting off to sea in butter-boats, hundreds of figures, to attract his thoughts; and yet that face of Marley, seven years dead, came like the ancient Prophet's rod, and swallowed up the whole. If each smooth tile had been a blank at first, with power to shape some picture on its surface from the disjointed fragments of his thoughts, there would have been a copy of old Marley's head on every one.

"Humbug!" said Scrooge; and walked across the room.

After several turns, he sat down again. As he threw his head back in the chair, his glance happened to rest upon a bell, a disused bell, that hung in the room, and communicated for some purpose now forgotten with a chamber, in the highest storey of the building. It was with great astonishment, and with a strange, inexplicable dread, that as he looked, he saw this bell begin to swing. It swung so softly in the outset that it scarcely made a sound; but soon it rang out loudly, and so did every bell in the house.

This might have lasted half a minute, or a minute, but it seemed an hour. The bells ceased as they had begun, together. They were succeeded by a clanking noise, deep down below; as if some person were dragging a heavy chain over the casks in the wine-merchant's cellar. Scrooge then remembered to have heard that ghosts in haunted houses were described as dragging chains.

The cellar-door flew open with a booming sound, and then he heard the noise much louder, on the floors below; then coming up the stairs; then coming straight towards his door.

" It's humbug still! " said Scrooge. " I won't believe it."

His colour changed though, when, without a pause, it came on through the heavy door, and passed into the room before his eyes. Upon its coming in, the dying flame leaped up, as though it cried, " I know him! Marley's Ghost! " and fell again.

The same face: the very same. Marley in his pigtail, usual waistcoat, tights and boots; the tassels on the latter bristling, like his pigtail, and his coat-skirts, and the hair upon his head. The chain he drew was clasped about his middle. It was long, and wound about him like a tail; and it was made (for Scrooge observed it closely) of cash-boxes, keys, padlocks, ledgers, deeds, and heavy purses wrought in steel. His body was transparent; so that Scrooge, observing him, and looking through his waistcoat, could see the two buttons on his coat behind.

Scrooge had often heard it said that Marley had no bowels, but he had never believed it until now.

No, nor did he believe it even now. Though he looked the phantom through and through, and saw it standing before him; though he felt the chilling influence of its death-cold eyes; and marked the very texture of the folded kerchief bound about its head and chin, which wrapper he had not observed before: he was still incredulous, and fought against his senses.

" How now! " said Scrooge, caustic and cold as ever. " What do you want with me? "

" Much! "—Marley's voice, no doubt about it.

" Who are you? "

" Ask me who I *was*."

" Who *were* you then? " said Scrooge, raising his voice. " You're particular—for a shade." He was going to say " *to* a shade," but substituted this, as more appropriate.

" In life I was your partner, Jacob Marley."

" Can you—can you sit down? " asked Scrooge, looking doubtfully at him.

" I can."

" Do it then."

Scrooge asked the question, because he didn't know whether a ghost so transparent might find himself in a condition to take a chair; and felt that in the event of its being impossible, it might involve the necessity of an embarrassing explanation. But the Ghost sat down on the opposite side of the fireplace, as if he were quite used to it.

"You don't believe in me," observed the Ghost.

" I don't," said Scrooge.

" What evidence would you have of my reality beyond that of your senses? "

" I don't know," said Scrooge.

" Why do you doubt your senses? "

" Because," said Scrooge, " a little thing affects them. A slight disorder of the stomach makes them cheats. You may be an undigested bit of beef, a blot of mustard, a crumb of cheese, a fragment of an underdone potato. There's more of gravy than of grave about you, whatever you are! "

Scrooge was not much in the habit of cracking jokes, nor did he feel, in his heart, by any means waggish then. The truth is, that he tried to be smart, as a means of distracting his own attention, and keeping down his terror; for the spectre's voice disturbed the very marrow in his bones.

To sit, staring at those fixed, glazed eyes, in silence for a moment, would play, Scrooge felt, the very deuce with him. There was something very awful, too, in the spectre's being provided with an infernal atmosphere of its own. Scrooge could not feel it himself, but this was clearly the case; for though the Ghost sat perfectly motionless, its hair, and skirts, and tassels, were still agitated as by the hot vapour from an oven.

" You see this toothpick?" said Scrooge, re-turning quickly to the charge, for the reason just assigned; and wishing, though it were only for a second, to divert the vision's stony gaze from himself.

" I do," replied the Ghost.

" You are not looking at it," said Scrooge.

" But I see it," said the Ghost, " notwith-standing."

" Well! " returned Scrooge. " I have but to swallow this, and be for the rest of my days per-secuted by a legion of goblins, all of my own creation. Humbug, I tell you—humbug! "

At this the spirit raised a frightful cry, and shook its chain with such a dismal and appalling noise, that Scrooge held on tight to his chair, to save himself from falling in a swoon. But how much greater was his horror, when the phantom taking off the bandage round its head, as if it were too warm to wear indoors, its lower jaw dropped down upon its breast!

Scrooge fell upon his knees, and clasped his hands before his face.

" Mercy! " he said. " Dreadful apparition, why do you trouble me? "

" Man of the worldly mind! " replied the Ghost, " do you believe in me or not? "

" I do," said Scrooge. " I must. But why do

B

spirits walk the earth, and why do they come to me? "

" It is required of every man," the Ghost returned, " that the spirit within him should walk abroad among his fellow-men, and travel far and wide; and if that spirit goes not forth in life, it is condemned to do so after death. It is doomed to wander through the world—oh, woe is me!—and witness what it cannot share, but might have shared on earth, and turned to happiness! "

Again the spectre raised a cry, and shook its chain, and wrung its shadowy hands.

" You are fettered," said Scrooge, trembling. " Tell me why? "

" I wear the chain I forged in life," replied the Ghost. " I made it link by link, and yard by yard; I girded it on of my own free will, and of my own free will I wore it. Is its pattern strange to *you*? "

Scrooge trembled more and more.

" Or would you know," pursued the Ghost, " the weight and length of the strong coil you bear yourself? It was full as heavy and as long as this, seven Christmas Eves ago. You have laboured on it, since. It is a ponderous chain! "

Scrooge glanced about him on the floor, in the expectation of finding himself surrounded by some fifty or sixty fathoms of iron cable: but he could see nothing.

"Jacob," he said imploringly. "Old Jacob Marley, tell me more. Speak comfort to me, Jacob."

"I have none to give," the Ghost replied. "It comes from other regions, Ebenezer Scrooge, and is conveyed by other ministers, to other kinds of men. Nor can I tell you what I would. A very little more is all permitted to me. I cannot rest, I cannot stay, I cannot linger anywhere. My spirit never walked beyond our counting-house —mark me!—in life my spirit never roved beyond the narrow limits of our money-changing hole; and weary journeys lie before me!"

It was a habit with Scrooge, whenever he became thoughtful, to put his hands in his breeches pockets. Pondering on what the Ghost had said, he did so now, but without lifting up his eyes, or getting off his knees.

"You must have been very slow about it, Jacob," Scrooge observed, in a business-like manner, though with humility and deference.

"Slow!" the Ghost repeated.

"Seven years dead," mused Scrooge. "And travelling all the time!"

"The whole time," said the Ghost. "No rest, no peace. Incessant torture of remorse."

" You travel fast? " said Scrooge.

" On the wings of the wind," replied the Ghost.

" You might have got over a great quantity of ground in seven years," said Scrooge.

The Ghost, on hearing this, set up another cry, and clanked its chain so hideously in the dead silence of the night, that the Ward would have been justified in indicting it for a nuisance.

" Oh! captive, bound, and doubled-ironed," cried the phantom, " not to know, that ages of incessant labour, by immortal creatures, for this earth must pass into eternity before the good of which it is susceptible is all developed. Not to know that any Christian spirit working kindly in its little sphere, whatever it may be, will find its mortal life too short for its vast means of usefulness. Not to know that no space of regret can make amends for one life's opportunity misused! Yet such was I! Oh! such was I!"

" But you were always a good man of business, Jacob," faltered Scrooge, who now began to apply this to himself.

" Business!" cried the Ghost, wringing its hands again. " Mankind was my business. The common welfare was my business; charity, mercy, forbearance, and benevolence, were, all, my business. The dealings of my trade were but a drop of water in the comprehensive ocean of my business!"

It held up its chain at arm's length, as if it were the cause of all its unavailing grief, and flung it heavily upon the ground again.

"At this time of the rolling year," the spectre said, "I suffer most. Why did I walk through crowds of fellow-beings with my eyes turned down, and never raise them to that blessed Star which led the Wise Men to a poor abode! Were there no poor homes to which its light would have conducted *me*!"

Scrooge was very much dismayed to hear the spectre going on at this rate, and began to quake exceedingly.

"Hear me!" cried the Ghost. "My time is nearly gone."

"I will," said Scrooge. "But don't be hard upon me! Don't be flowery, Jacob! Pray!"

"How it is that I appear before you in a shape that you can see, I may not tell. I have sat invisible beside you many and many a day."

It was not an agreeable idea. Scrooge shivered, and wiped the perspiration from his brow.

"That is no light part of my penance," pursued the Ghost. "I am here to-night to warn you, that you have yet a chance and hope of escaping my fate. A chance and hope of my procuring, Ebenezer."

" You were always a good friend to me," said Scrooge. " Thank'ee! "

" You will be haunted," resumed the Ghost, " by Three Spirits."

Scrooge's countenance fell almost as low as the Ghost's had done.

" Is that the chance and hope you mentioned, Jacob? " he demanded, in a faltering voice.

" It is."

" I—I think I'd rather not," said Scrooge.

" Without their visits," said the Ghost, " you cannot hope to shun the path I tread. Expect the first to-morrow, when the bell tolls one."

" Couldn't I take 'em all at once, and have it over, Jacob? " hinted Scrooge.

" Expect the second on the next night at the same hour. The third upon the next night when the last stroke of twelve has ceased to vibrate. Look to see me no more; and look that, for your own sake, you remember what has passed between us! "

When it had said these words, the spectre took its wrapper from the table, and bound it round its head, as before. Scrooge knew this, by the smart sound its teeth made, when the jaws were brought together by the bandage. He ventured

to raise his eyes again, and found his supernatural visitor confronting him in an erect attitude, with its chain wound over and about its
arm.

The apparition walked backward from him;
and at every step it took, the window raised
itself a little, so that when the spectre reached
it, it was wide open. It beckoned Scrooge to
approach, which he did. When they were within
two paces of each other, Marley's Ghost held up
its hand, warning him to come no nearer. Scrooge
stopped.

Not so much in obedience, as in surprise and
fear: for on the raising of the hand, he became
sensible of confused noises in the air; incoherent
sounds of lamentation and regret; wailings inexpressibly sorrowful and self-accusatory. The
spectre, after listening for a moment, joined in
the mournful dirge; and floated out upon the
bleak, dark night.

Scrooge followed to the window: desperate in
his curiosity. He looked out.

The air was filled with phantoms, wandering
hither and thither in restless haste, and moaning
as they went. Every one of them wore chains
like Marley's Ghost; some few (they might be
guilty governments) were linked together; none
were free. Many had been personally known to

Scrooge in their lives. He had been quite familiar with one old ghost, in a white waistcoat, with a monstrous iron safe attached to its ankle, who cried piteously at being unable to assist a wretched woman with an infant, whom it saw below, upon a door-step. The misery with them all was, clearly, that they sought to interfere, for good, in human matters, and had lost the power for ever.

Whether these creatures faded into mist, or mist enshrouded them, he could not tell. But they and their spirit voices faded together; and the night became as it had been when he walked home.

Scrooge closed the window, and examined the door by which the Ghost had entered. It was double-locked, as he had locked it with his own hands, and the bolts were undisturbed. He tried to say " Humbug!" but stopped at the first syllable. And being, from the emotion he had undergone, or the fatigues of the day, or his glimpse of the Invisible World, or the dull conversation of the Ghost, or the lateness of the hour, much in need of repose; went straight to bed, without undressing, and fell asleep upon the instant.

Stave Two
The first of the three Spirits

A lonely boy was reading —

WHEN Scrooge awoke, it was so dark, that looking out of bed, he could scarcely distinguish the transparent window from the opaque walls of his chamber. He was endeavouring to pierce the darkness with his ferret eyes, when the chimes of a neighbouring church struck the four quarters. So he listened for the hour.

To his great astonishment the heavy bell went on from six to seven, and from seven to eight, and regularly up to twelve; then stopped. Twelve! It was past two when he went to bed. The clock was wrong. An icicle must have got into the works. Twelve!

He touched the spring of his repeater, to correct this most preposterous clock. Its rapid little pulse beat twelve; and stopped.

"Why, it isn't possible," said Scrooge, "that I can have slept through a whole day and far into another night. It isn't possible that anything has happened to the sun, and this is twelve at noon!"

The idea being an alarming one, he scrambled out of bed, and groped his way to the window. He was obliged to rub the frost off with the sleeve of his dressing-gown before he could see anything; and could see very little then. All he could make out was, that it was still very foggy and extremely cold, and that there was no noise of people running to and fro, and making a great stir, as there unquestionably would have been if night had beaten off bright day, and taken possession of the world. This was a great relief, because "three days after sight of this First of Exchange pay to Mr. Ebenezer Scrooge or his order," and so forth, would have become a mere

United States security if there were no days to count by.

Scrooge went to bed again, and thought, and thought, and thought it over and over and over, and could make nothing of it. The more he thought, the more perplexed he was; and the more he endeavoured not to think, the more he thought. Marley's Ghost bothered him exceedingly. Every time he resolved within himself, after mature inquiry, that it was all a dream, his mind flew back again, like a strong spring released, to its first position, and presented the same problem to be worked all through, " Was it a dream or not? "

Scrooge lay in this state until the chimes had gone three quarters more, when he remembered on a sudden, that the Ghost had warned him of a visitation when the bell tolled one. He resolved to lie awake until the hour was passed; and, considering that he could no more go to sleep than go to Heaven, this was perhaps the wisest resolution in his power.

The quarter was so long, that he was more than once convinced he must have sunk into a doze unconsciously, and missed the clock. At length it broke upon his listening ear.

" Ding, dong! "

" A quarter past," said Scrooge, counting.

" Ding, dong! "

" Half past! " said Scrooge.

" Ding, dong! "

" A quarter to it," said Scrooge.

" Ding, dong! "

" The hour itself," said Scrooge, triumphantly, " and nothing else! "

He spoke before the hour bell sounded, which it now did with a deep, dull, hollow, melancholy ONE. Light flashed up in the room upon the instant, and the curtains of his bed were drawn.

The curtains of his bed were drawn aside, I tell you, by a hand. Not the curtains at his feet, nor the curtains at his back, but those to which his face was addressed. The curtains of his bed were drawn aside; and Scrooge, starting up into a half-recumbent attitude, found himself face to face with the unearthly visitor who drew them: as close to it as I am now to you, and I am standing in the spirit at your elbow.

It was a strange figure—like a child: yet not so like a child as like an old man, viewed through some supernatural medium, which gave him the appearance of having receded from the view, and being diminished to a child's proportions. Its hair, which hung about its neck and down its back, was white as if with age; and yet the face

had not a wrinkle in it, and the tenderest bloom
was on the skin. The arms were very long and
muscular; the hands the same, as if its hold were
of uncommon strength. Its legs and feet, most
delicately formed, were, like those upper members, bare. It wore a tunic of the purest white;
and round its waist was bound a lustrous belt,
the sheen of which was beautiful. It held a
branch of fresh green holly in its hand; and, in
singular contradiction of that wintry emblem,
had its dress trimmed with summer flowers.
But the strangest thing about it was, that from
the crown of its head there sprang a bright clear
jet of light, by which all this was visible; and
which was doubtless the occasion of its using,
in its duller moments, a great extinguisher for
a cap, which it now held under its arm.

Even this, though, when Scrooge looked at it
with increasing steadiness, was *not* its strangest
quality. For as its belt sparkled and glittered
now in one part and now in another, and what
was light one instant, at another time was dark,
so the figure itself fluctuated in its distinctness:
being now a thing with one arm, now with one
leg, now with twenty legs, now a pair of legs without a head, now a head without a body: of which
dissolving parts, no outline would be visible in
the dense gloom wherein they melted away. And

in the very wonder of this, it would be itself again; distinct and clear as ever.

" Are you the Spirit, sir, whose coming was foretold to me? " asked Scrooge.

" I am! "

The voice was soft and gentle. Singularly low, as if instead of being so close beside him, it were at a distance.

" Who, and what are you? " Scrooge demanded.

" I am the Ghost of Christmas Past."

" Long past? " inquired Scrooge: observant of its dwarfish stature.

" No. Your past."

Perhaps, Scrooge could not have told anybody why, if anybody could have asked him; but he had a special desire to see the Spirit in his cap; and begged him to be covered.

" What! " exclaimed the Ghost, " would you so soon put out, with worldly hands, the light I give? Is it not enough that you are one of those whose passions made this cap, and force me through whole trains of years to wear it low upon my brow! "

Scrooge reverently disclaimed all intention to offend, or any knowledge of having wilfully " bonneted " the Spirit at any period of his life. He then made bold to inquire what business brought him there.

" Your welfare! " said the Ghost.

Scrooge expressed himself much obliged, but could not help thinking that a night of unbroken rest would have been more conducive to that end. The Spirit must have heard him thinking, for it said immediately:

" Your reclamation, then. Take heed! "

It put out its strong hand as it spoke, and clasped him gently by the arm.

" Rise! and walk with me! "

It would have been in vain for Scrooge to plead that the weather and the hour were not adapted to pedestrian purposes; that bed was warm, and the thermometer a long way below freezing; that he was clad but lightly in his slippers, dressing-gown, and nightcap; and that he had a cold upon him at that time. The grasp, though gentle as a woman's hand, was not to be resisted. He rose: but finding that the Spirit made towards the window, clasped its robe in supplication.

" I am a mortal," Scrooge remonstrated, " and liable to fall."

" Bear but a touch of my hand *there*," said the Spirit, laying it upon his heart, " and you shall be upheld in more than this! "

As the words were spoken, they passed through the wall, and stood upon an open country road, with fields on either hand. The city had entirely vanished. Not a vestige of it was to be seen. The darkness and the mist had vanished with it, for it was a clear, cold, winter day, with snow upon the ground.

"Good Heaven!" said Scrooge, clasping his hands together, as he looked about him. " I was bred in this place. I was a boy here!"

The Spirit gazed upon him mildly. Its gentle touch, though it had been light and instantaneous, appeared still present to the old man's sense of feeling. He was conscious of a thousand odours floating in the air, each one connected with a thousand thoughts, and hopes, and joys, and cares long, long forgotten!

" Your lip is trembling," said the Ghost. "And what is that upon your cheek?"

Scrooge muttered, with an unusual catching in his voice, that it was a pimple; and begged the Ghost to lead him where he would.

" You recollect the way?" inquired the Spirit.

" Remember it!" cried Scrooge with fervour —" I could walk it blindfold."

" Strange to have forgotten it for so many years!" observed the Ghost. " Let us go on."

They walked along the road; Scrooge recognising every gate, and post, and tree; until a little market-town appeared in the distance, with its bridge, its church, and winding river. Some shaggy ponies now were seen trotting towards them with boys upon their backs, who called to other boys in country gigs and carts, driven by farmers. All these boys were in great spirits, and shouted to each other, until the broad fields were so full of merry music, that the crisp air laughed to hear it.

"These are but shadows of the things that have been," said the Ghost. "They have no consciousness of us."

The jocund travellers came on; and as they came, Scrooge knew and named them every one. Why was he rejoiced beyond all bounds to see them! Why did his cold eye glisten, and his heart leap up as they went past! Why was he filled with gladness when he heard them give each other Merry Christmas, as they parted at cross-roads and bye-ways, for their several homes! What was merry Christmas to Scrooge? Out upon merry Christmas! What good had it ever done to him?

"The school is not quite deserted," said the Ghost. "A solitary child, neglected by his friends, is left there still."

Scrooge said he knew it. And he sobbed.

They left the high-road, by a well-remembered lane, and soon approached a mansion of dull red brick, with a little weathercock-surmounted cupola on the roof, and a bell hanging in it. It was a large house, but one of broken fortunes; for the spacious offices were little used, their walls were damp and mossy, their windows broken, and their gates decayed. Fowls clucked and strutted in the stables; and the coach-houses and sheds were overrun with grass. Nor was it more retentive of its ancient state, within; for entering the dreary hall, and glancing through the open doors of many rooms, they found them poorly furnished, cold, and vast. There was an earthy savour in the air, a chilly bareness in the place, which associated itself somehow with too much getting up by candle-light, and not too much to eat.

They went, the Ghost and Scrooge, across the hall, to a door at the back of the house. It opened before them, and disclosed a long, bare, melancholy room, made barer still by lines of plain deal forms and desks. At one of these a lonely boy was reading near a feeble fire; and Scrooge sat down upon a form, and wept to see his poor forgotten self as he had used to be.

Not a latent echo in the house, not a squeak and scuffle from the mice behind the panelling, not a drip from the half-thawed water-spout in the dull yard behind, not a sigh among the leafless boughs of one despondent poplar, not the idle swinging of an empty store-house door, no, not a clicking in the fire, but fell upon the heart of Scrooge with softening influence, and gave a freer passage to his tears.

The Spirit touched him on the arm, and pointed to his younger self, intent upon his reading. Suddenly a man, in foreign garments: wonderfully real and distinct to look at: stood outside the window, with an axe stuck in his belt, and leading an ass laden with wood by the bridle.

"Why, it's Ali Baba!" Scrooge exclaimed in ecstasy. "It's dear old honest Ali Baba! Yes, yes, I know! One Christmas time, when yonder solitary child was left here all alone, he *did* come, for the first time, just like that. Poor boy! And Valentine," said Scrooge, "and his wild brother, Orson; there they go! And what's his name, who was put down in his drawers, asleep, at the Gate of Damascus; don't you see him! And the Sultan's Groom turned upside down by the Genii; there he is upon his head! Serve him right. I'm glad of it. What business had *he* to be married to the Princess!"

To hear Scrooge expending all the earnestness of his nature on such subjects, in a most extraordinary voice between laughing and crying; and to see his heightened and excited face; would have been a surprise to his business friends in the City, indeed.

" There's the Parrot! " cried Scrooge. " Green body and yellow tail, with a thing like a lettuce growing out of the top of his head; there he is! Poor Robin Crusoe, he called him, when he came home again after sailing round the island. ' Poor Robin Crusoe, where have you been, Robin Crusoe? ' The man thought he was dreaming, but he wasn't. It was the Parrot, you know. There goes Friday, running for his life to the little creek! Halloa! Hoop! Halloo! "

Then, with a rapidity of transition very foreign to his usual character, he said, in pity for his former self, " Poor boy! " and cried again.

" I wish," Scrooge muttered, putting his hand in his pocket, and looking about him, after drying his eyes with his cuff: " but it's too late now."

" What is the matter? " asked the Spirit.

" Nothing," said Scrooge. " Nothing. There was a boy singing a Christmas Carol at my door last night. I should like to have given him some-thing: that's all."

The Ghost smiled thoughtfully, and waved its hand: saying as it did so, " Let us see another Christmas! "

Scrooge's former self grew larger at the words, and the room became a little darker and more dirty. The panels shrank, the windows cracked; fragments of plaster fell out of the ceiling, and the naked laths were shown instead; but how all this was brought about, Scrooge knew no more than you do. He only knew that it was quite correct; that everything had happened so; that there he was, alone again, when all the other boys had gone home for the jolly holidays.

He was not reading now, but walking up and down despairingly. Scrooge looked at the Ghost, and with a mournful shaking of his head, glanced anxiously towards the door.

It opened; and a little girl, much younger than the boy, came darting in, and putting her arms about his neck, and often kissing him, addressed him as her " Dear, dear brother."

" I have come to bring you home, dear brother! " said the child, clapping her tiny hands, and bending down to laugh. " To bring you home, home, home! "

" Home, little Fan? " returned the boy.

" Yes! " said the child, brimful of glee. " Home, for good and all. Home, for ever and ever. Father is so much kinder than he used to be, that home's like Heaven! He spoke so gently to me one dear night when I was going to bed, that I was not afraid to ask him once more if you might come home; and he said Yes, you should; and sent me in a coach to bring you. And you're to be a man!" said the child, opening her eyes, "and are never to come back here; but first, we're to be together all the Christmas long, and have the merriest time in all the world."

"You are quite a woman, little Fan!" exclaimed the boy.

She clapped her hands and laughed, and tried to touch his head; but being too little, laughed again, and stood on tiptoe to embrace him. Then she began to drag him, in her childish eagerness, towards the door; and he, nothing loth to go, accompanied her.

A terrible voice in the hall cried, "Bring down Master Scrooge's box, there!" and in the hall appeared the schoolmaster himself, who glared on Master Scrooge with a ferocious condescension, and threw him into a dreadful state of mind by shaking hands with him. He then conveyed him and his sister into the veriest old well of a shivering best-parlour that ever was seen, where the maps upon the wall, and the celestial and terrestrial globes in the windows, were waxy with cold. Here he produced a decanter of curiously light wine, and a block of curiously heavy cake, and administered instalments of those dainties to the young people: at the same time, sending out a meagre servant to offer a glass of " some-

Administered instalments of these dainties

thing" to the postboy, who answered that he
thanked the gentleman, but if it was the same
tap as he had tasted before, he had rather not.
Master Scrooge's trunk being by this time tied
on to the top of the chaise, the children bade the
schoolmaster good-bye right willingly; and getting into it, drove gaily down the garden sweep:
the quick wheels dashing the hoar-frost and snow
from off the dark leaves of the evergreens like spray.

"Always a delicate creature, whom a breath

might have withered," said the Ghost. " But she had a large heart! "

" So she had," cried Scrooge. " You're right. I'll not gainsay it, Spirit. God forbid! "

" She died a woman," said the Ghost, " and had, as I think, children."

" One child," Scrooge returned.

" True," said the Ghost. " Your nephew! "

Scrooge seemed uneasy in his mind; and answered briefly, " Yes."

Although they had but that moment left the school behind them, they were now in the busy thoroughfares of a city, where shadowy passengers passed and re-passed; where shadowy carts and coaches battled for the way, and all the strife and tumult of a real city were. It was made plain enough, by the dressing of the shops, that here too it was Christmas time again; but it was evening, and the streets were lighted up.

The Ghost stopped at a certain warehouse door, and asked Scrooge if he knew it.

" Know it! " said Scrooge. " Was I apprenticed here? "

They went in. At sight of an old gentleman in a Welsh wig, sitting behind such a high desk, that if he had been two inches taller he must have knocked his head against the ceiling, Scrooge cried in great excitement:

" Why, it's old Fezziwig! Bless his heart; it's Fezziwig alive again! "

Old Fezziwig laid down his pen, and looked up at the clock, which pointed to the hour of seven. He rubbed his hands; adjusted his capacious waistcoat; laughed all over himself, from his shoes to his organ of benevolence; and called out in a comfortable, oily, rich, fat, jovial voice:

" Yo ho, there! Ebenezer! Dick! "

Scrooge's former self, now grown a young man, came briskly in, accompanied by his fellow-'prentice.

" Dick Wilkins, to be sure! " said Scrooge to the Ghost. " Bless me, yes. There he is. He was very much attached to me, was Dick. Poor Dick! Dear, dear! "

" Yo ho, my boys! " said Fezziwig. " No more work to-night. Christmas Eve, Dick. Christmas, Ebenezer! Let's have the shutters up," cried old Fezziwig, with a sharp clap of his hands, " before a man can say Jack Robinson! "

You wouldn't believe how those two fellows went at it! They charged into the street with the shutters — one, two, three — had 'em up in their places — four, five, six — barred 'em and pinned 'em—seven, eight, nine—and came back before you could have got to twelve, panting like racehorses.

" Hilli-ho! " cried old Fezziwig, skipping down from the high desk, with wonderful agility. " Clear away, my lads, and let's have lots of room here! Hilli-ho, Dick! Chirrup, Ebenezer! "

Clear away! There was nothing they wouldn't have cleared away, or couldn't have cleared away, with old Fezziwig looking on. It was done in a minute. Every movable was packed off, as if it were dismissed from public life for evermore; the floor was swept and watered, the lamps were trimmed, fuel was heaped upon the fire; and the warehouse was as snug, and warm, and dry, and bright a ballroom, as you would desire to see upon a winter's night.

In came a fiddler with a music-book, and went up to the lofty desk, and made an orchestra of it, and tuned like fifty stomach-aches. In came Mrs. Fezziwig, one vast substantial smile. In came the three Miss Fezziwigs, beaming and lovable. In came the six young followers whose hearts they broke. In came all the young men and women employed in the business. In came the housemaid, with her cousin, the baker. In came the cook, with her brother's particular friend, the milkman. In came the boy from over the way, who was suspected of not having board enough from his master; trying to hide himself behind the girl from next door but one, who was proved to have had her ears pulled by her mistress. In they all came, one after another; some shyly, some boldly, some gracefully, some awkwardly, some pushing, some pulling; in they all came, anyhow and everyhow. Away they all went, twenty couple at once, hands half round and back again the other way; down the middle and up again; round and round in various stages of affectionate grouping; old top couple always turning up in the wrong place; new top couple starting off again, as soon as they got there; all top couples at last, and not a bottom one to help them. When this result was brought about, old Fezziwig, clapping his hands to stop the dance, cried out, " Well done! " and the fiddler plunged his hot face into a pot of porter, especially provided for that purpose. But scorning rest upon his re-appearance, he instantly began again, though there were no dancers yet, as if the other fiddler had been carried home, exhausted, on a shutter; and he were a bran-new man resolved to beat him out of sight, or perish.

There were more dances, and there were forfeits, and more dances, and there was cake, and there was negus, and there was a great piece of Cold Roast, and there was a great piece of Cold Boiled, and there were mince-pies, and plenty of beer. But the great effect of the evening came

after the Roast and Boiled, when the fiddler
(an artful dog, mind! The sort of man who knew
his business better than you or I could have told
it him!) struck up "Sir Roger de Coverley."
Then old Fezziwig stood out to dance with Mrs.
Fezziwig. Top couple, too; with a good stiff
piece of work cut out for them; three or four
and twenty pair of partners; people who were
not to be trifled with; people who *would* dance,
and had no notion of walking.

But if they had been twice as many: ah, four
times: old Fezziwig would have been a match
for them, and so would Mrs. Fezziwig. As to *her*,
she was worthy to be his partner in every sense
of the term. If that's not high praise, tell me
higher, and I'll use it. A positive light appeared
to issue from Fezziwig's calves. They shone in
every part of the dance like moons. You couldn't
have predicted, at any given time, what would
become of 'em next. And when old Fezziwig and
Mrs. Fezziwig had gone all through the dance;
advance and retire, hold hands with your partner;
bow and curtsey; corkscrew; thread-the-needle
and back again to your place; Fezziwig " cut "
—cut so deftly, that he appeared to wink with
his legs, and came upon his feet again without
a stagger.

When the clock struck eleven, this domestic

ball broke up. Mr. and Mrs. Fezziwig took their stations, one on either side the door, and shaking hands with every person individually as he or she went out, wished him or her a Merry Christmas. When everybody had retired but the two 'prentices, they did the same to them; and thus the cheerful voices died away, and the lads were left to their beds; which were under a counter in the back-shop.

During the whole of this time, Scrooge had acted like a man out of his wits. His heart and soul were in the scene, and with his former self. He corroborated everything, remembered everything, enjoyed everything, and underwent the strangest agitation. It was not until now, when the bright faces of his former self and Dick were turned from them, that he remembered the Ghost, and became conscious that it was looking full upon him, while the light upon its head burnt very clear.

" A small matter," said the Ghost, " to make these silly folks so full of gratitude."

" Small! " echoed Scrooge.

The Spirit signed to him to listen to the two apprentices, who were pouring out their hearts in praise of Fezziwig: and when he had done so, said,—

" Why! Is it not? He has spent but a few

pounds of your mortal money: three or four, perhaps. Is that so much that he deserves this praise?"

"It isn't that," said Scrooge, heated by the remark, and speaking unconsciously like his former, not his latter, self. "It isn't that, Spirit. He has the power to render us happy or unhappy; to make our service light or burdensome; a pleasure or a toil. Say that his power lies in words and looks; in things so slight and insignificant that it is impossible to add and count 'em up: what then? The happiness he gives, is quite as great as if it cost a fortune."

He felt the Spirit's glance, and stopped.

"What is the matter?" asked the Ghost.

"Nothing particular," said Scrooge.

"Something, I think?" the Ghost insisted.

"No," said Scrooge, "no. I should like to be able to say a word or two to my clerk just now! That's all."

His former self turned down the lamps as he gave utterance to the wish; and Scrooge and the Ghost again stood side by side in the open air.

"My time grows short," observed the Spirit. "Quick!"

This was not addressed to Scrooge, or to any one whom he could see, but it produced an immediate effect. For again Scrooge saw himself. He was older now; a man in the prime of life. His face had not the harsh and rigid lines of later years; but it had begun to wear the signs of care and avarice. There was an eager, greedy, restless motion in the eye, which showed the passion that had taken root, and where the shadow of the growing tree would fall.

He was not alone, but sat by the side of a fair young girl in a mourning-dress: in whose eyes there were tears, which sparkled in the light that shone out of the Ghost of Christmas Past.

" It matters little," she said softly. " To you, very little. Another idol has displaced me; and if it can cheer and comfort you in time to come, as I would have tried to do, I have no just cause to grieve."

" What Idol has displaced you? " he rejoined.

" A golden one."

" This is the even-handed dealing of the world!" he said. " There is nothing on which it is so hard as poverty; and there is nothing it professes to condemn with such severity as the pursuit of wealth! "

" You fear the world too much," she answered gently. " All your other hopes have merged into the hope of being beyond the chance of its sordid reproach. I have seen your nobler aspirations fall off one by one, until the master-passion, Gain, engrosses you. Have I not?"

"What then?" he retorted. "Even if I have grown so much wiser, what then? I am not changed towards you."

She shook her head.

"Am I?"

"Our contract is an old one. It was made when we were both poor and content to be so, until, in good season, we could improve our worldly fortune by our patient industry. You *are* changed. When it was made, you were another man."

"I was a boy," he said impatiently.

"Your own feeling tells you that you were not what you are," she returned. "I am. That which promised happiness when we were one in heart, is fraught with misery now that we are two. How often and how keenly I have thought of this, I will not say. It is enough that I *have* thought of it, and can release you."

"Have I ever sought release?"

"In words. No. Never."

"In what, then?"

"In a changed nature; in an altered spirit; in another atmosphere of life; another Hope as its great end. In everything that made my love of any worth or value in your sight. If this had never been between us," said the girl, looking mildly, but with steadiness, upon him; " tell me, would you seek me out and try to win me now? Ah, no! "

He seemed to yield to the justice of this supposition, in spite of himself. But he said with a struggle, " You think not."

" I would gladly think otherwise if I could," she answered, " Heaven knows! When *I* have learned a Truth like this, I know how strong and irresistible it must be. But if you were free to-day, to-morrow, yesterday, can even I believe that you would choose a dowerless girl—you who, in your very confidence with her, weigh everything by Gain: or, choosing her, if for a moment you were false enough to your one guiding principle to do so, do I not know that your repentance and regret would surely follow? I do; and I release you. With a full heart, for the love of him you once were."

He was about to speak; but with her head turned from him, she resumed.

" You may—the memory of what is past half makes me hope you will—have pain in this. A very, very brief time, and you will dismiss the recollection of it, gladly, as an unprofitable dream, from which it happened well that you awoke. May you be happy in the life you have chosen! "

c

She left him, and they parted.

"Spirit!" said Scrooge, "show me no more! Conduct me home. Why do you delight to torture me?"

"One shadow more!" exclaimed the Ghost.

"No more!" cried Scrooge. "No more. I don't wish to see it. Show me no more!"

But the relentless Ghost pinioned him in both his arms, and forced him to observe what happened next.

They were in another scene and place; a room, not very large or handsome, but full of comfort. Near to the winter fire sat a beautiful young girl, so like the last that Scrooge believed it was the same, until he saw *her*, now a comely matron, sitting opposite her daughter. The noise in this room was perfectly tumultuous, for there were more children there than Scrooge in his agitated state of mind could count; and, unlike the celebrated herd in the poem, they were not forty children conducting themselves like one, but every child was conducting itself like forty. The consequences were uproarious beyond belief; but no one seemed to care; on the contrary, the mother and daughter laughed heartily, and enjoyed it very much; and the latter, soon beginning to mingle in the sports, got pillaged by the young brigands most ruthlessly. What would I

not have given to be one of them! Though I
never could have been so rude, no, no! I wouldn't
for the wealth of all the world have crushed
that braided hair, and torn it down; and for
the precious little shoe, I wouldn't have plucked
it off, God bless my soul! to save my life. As
to measuring her waist in sport, as they did, bold
young brood, I couldn't have done it; I should
have expected my arm to have grown round it
for a punishment, and never come straight again.
And yet I should have dearly liked, I own, to
have touched her lips; to have questioned her,
that she might have opened them; to have looked
upon the lashes of her downcast eyes, and
never raised a blush; to have let loose waves
of hair, an inch of which would be a keepsake
beyond price: in short, I should have liked, I
do confess, to have had the lightest licence of a
child, and yet been man enough to know its
value.

But now a knocking at the door was heard,
and such a rush immediately ensued that she with
laughing face and plundered dress was borne towards it the centre of a flushed and boisterous
group, just in time to greet the father, who came
home attended by a man laden with Christmas
toys and presents. Then the shouting and the
struggling, and the onslaught that was made on

the defenceless porter! The scaling him with chairs for ladders to dive into his pockets, despoil him of brown-paper parcels, hold on tight by his cravat, hug him round the neck, pommel his back, and kick his legs in irrepressible affection! The shouts of wonder and delight with which the development of every package was received! The terrible announcement that the baby had been taken in the act of putting a doll's frying-pan into his mouth, and was more than suspected of having swallowed a fictitious turkey, glued on a wooden platter! The immense relief of finding this a false alarm! The joy, and gratitude, and ecstasy! They are all indescribable alike. It is enough that by degrees the children and their emotions got out of the parlour, and by one stair at a time, up to the top of the house; where they went to bed, and so subsided.

And now Scrooge looked on more attentively than ever, when the master of the house, having his daughter leaning fondly on him, sat down with her and her mother at his own fireside; and when he thought that such another creature, quite as graceful and as full of promise, might have called him father, and been a spring-time in the haggard winter of his life, his sight grew very dim indeed.

" Belle," said the husband, turning to his wife

with a smile, " I saw an old friend of yours this afternoon."

" Who was it? "

" Guess! "

" How can I? Tut, don't I know? " she added in the same breath, laughing as he laughed. " Mr. Scrooge."

" Mr. Scrooge it was. I passed his office window; and as it was not shut up, and he had a candle inside, I could scarcely help seeing him. His partner lies upon the point of death, I hear, and there he sat alone. Quite alone in the world, I do believe."

" Spirit! " said Scrooge in a broken voice, " remove me from this place."

" I told you these were shadows of the things that have been," said the Ghost. " That they are what they are, do not blame me! "

" Remove me! " Scrooge exclaimed, " I cannot bear it! "

He turned upon the Ghost, and seeing that it looked upon him with a face, in which in some strange way there were fragments of all the faces it had shown him, wrestled with it.

" Leave me! Take me back. Haunt me no longer! "

In the struggle, if that can be called a struggle in which the Ghost with no visible resistance on its own part was undisturbed by any effort of its adversary, Scrooge observed that its light was burning high and bright; and dimly connecting that with its influence over him, he seized the extinguisher-cap, and by a sudden action pressed it down upon its head.

The Spirit dropped beneath it, so that the extinguisher covered its whole form; but though Scrooge pressed it down with all his force, he could not hide the light, which streamed from under it, in an unbroken flood upon the ground.

He was conscious of being exhausted, and overcome by an irresistible drowsiness; and, further, of being in his own bedroom. He gave the cap a parting squeeze, in which his hand relaxed; and had barely time to reel to bed, before he sank into a heavy sleep.

Stave Three
The second of the three Spirits

C. Brock 1905

Oh, a wonderful pudding!

AWAKING in the middle of a prodigiously tough snore, and sitting up in bed to get his thoughts together, Scrooge had no occasion to be told that the bell was again upon the stroke of One. He felt that he was restored to consciousness in the right nick of time, for the especial purpose of holding a conference with the second messenger despatched to him through Jacob Marley's intervention. But, finding that he turned uncomfortably cold when he began to

wonder which of his curtains this new spectre
would draw back, he put them every one aside
with his own hands, and lying down again, estab-
lished a sharp look-out all round the bed. For
he wished to challenge the Spirit on the moment
of its appearance, and did not wish to be taken
by surprise and made nervous.

Gentlemen of the free-and-easy sort, who
plume themselves on being acquainted with a
move or two, and being usually equal to the time-
of-day, express the wide range of their capacity
for adventure by observing that they are good
for anything from pitch-and-toss to manslaughter;
between which opposite extremes, no doubt, there
lies a tolerably wide and comprehensive range of
subjects. Without venturing for Scrooge quite as
hardily as this, I don't mind calling on you to
believe that he was ready for a good broad field
of strange appearances, and that nothing between
a baby and a rhinoceros would have astonished
him very much.

Now, being prepared for almost anything, he
was not by any means prepared for nothing; and,
consequently, when the bell struck One, and no
shape appeared, he was taken with a violent fit
of trembling. Five minutes, ten minutes, a
quarter of an hour went by, yet nothing came.
All this time, he lay upon his bed, the very core

and centre of a blaze of ruddy light, which streamed upon it when the clock proclaimed the hour; and which, being only light, was more alarming than a dozen ghosts, as he was powerless to make out what it meant, or would be at; and was sometimes apprehensive that he might be at that very moment an interesting case of spontaneous combustion, without having the consolation of knowing it. At last, however, he began to think—as you or I would have thought at first; for it is always the person not in the predicament who knows what ought to have been done in it, and would unquestionably have done it too—at last, I say, he began to think that the source and secret of this ghostly light might be in the adjoining room, from whence, on further tracing it, it seemed to shine. This idea taking full possession of his mind, he got up softly and shuffled in his slippers to the door.

The moment Scrooge's hand was on the lock, a strange voice called him by his name, and bade him enter. He obeyed.

It was his own room. There was no doubt about that. But it had undergone a surprising transformation. The walls and ceiling were so hung with living green, that it looked a perfect grove, from every part of which, bright gleaming berries glistened. The crisp leaves of holly,

*c

mistletoe, and ivy reflected back the light, as if so many little mirrors had been scattered there; and such a mighty blaze went roaring up the chimney, as that dull petrifaction of a hearth had never known in Scrooge's time, or Marley's, or for many and many a winter season gone. Heaped up on the floor, to form a kind of throne, were turkeys, geese, game, poultry, brawn, great joints of meat, sucking-pigs, long wreaths of sausages, mince-pies, plum-puddings, barrels of oysters, red-hot chestnuts, cherry-cheeked apples, juicy oranges, luscious pears, immense twelfth-cakes, and seething bowls of punch, that made the chamber dim with their delicious steam. In easy state upon this couch, there sat a jolly Giant, glorious to see; who bore a glowing torch, in shape not unlike Plenty's horn, and held it up, high up, to shed its light on Scrooge, as he came peeping round the door.

"Come in!" exclaimed the Ghost. "Come in! and know me better, man!"

Scrooge entered timidly, and hung his head before this Spirit. He was not the dogged Scrooge he had been; and though the Spirit's eyes were clear and kind, he did not like to meet them.

"I am the Ghost of Christmas Present," said the Spirit. "Look upon me!"

Scrooge reverently did so. It was clothed in one

simple deep green robe, or mantle, bordered with white fur. This garment hung so loosely on the figure, that its capacious breast was bare, as if disdaining to be warded or concealed by any artifice. Its feet, observable beneath the ample folds of the garment, were also bare; and on its head it wore no other covering than a holly wreath set here and there with shining icicles. Its dark brown curls were long and free; free as its genial face, its sparkling eye, its open hand, its cheery voice, its unconstrained demeanour, and its joyful air. Girded round its middle was an antique scabbard; but no sword was in it, and the ancient sheath was eaten up with rust.

" You have never seen the like of me before! " exclaimed the Spirit.

" Never," Scrooge made answer to it.

" Have never walked forth with the younger members of my family; meaning (for I am very young) my elder brothers born in these later years? " pursued the Phantom.

" I don't think I have," said Scrooge. " I am afraid I have not. Have you had many brothers, Spirit? "

" More than eighteen hundred," said the Ghost.

" A tremendous family to provide for! " muttered Scrooge.

The Ghost of Christmas Present rose.

" Spirit," said Scrooge, submissively, " conduct me where you will. I went forth last night on compulsion, and I learnt a lesson which is working now. To-night, if you have aught to teach me, let me profit by it."

" Touch my robe! "

Scrooge did as he was told, and held it fast.

Holly, mistletoe, red berries, ivy, turkeys, geese, game, poultry, brawn, meat, pigs, sausages, oysters, pies, puddings, fruit, and punch, all vanished instantly. So did the room, the fire, the ruddy glow, the hour of night, and they stood in the City streets on Christmas morning, where (for the weather was severe) the people made a rough, but brisk and not unpleasant kind of music, in scraping the snow from the pavement in front of their dwellings, and from the tops of their houses: whence it was mad delight to the boys to see it come plumping down into the road below, and splitting into artificial little snow-storms.

The house fronts looked black enough, and the windows blacker, contrasting with the smooth white sheet of snow upon the roofs, and with the dirtier snow upon the ground; which last deposit had been ploughed up in deep furrows by the heavy wheels of carts and waggons; furrows that crossed and recrossed each other hundreds of times where the great streets branched off, and made intricate channels, hard to trace, in the thick yellow mud and icy water. The sky was gloomy, and the shortest streets were choked up with a dingy mist, half thawed half frozen, whose heavier particles descended in a shower of sooty atoms, as if all the chimneys in Great Britain had, by one consent, caught fire, and were blazing away to their dear hearts' content. There was nothing very cheerful in the climate or the town, and yet was there an air of cheerfulness abroad that the clearest summer air and brightest summer sun might have endeavoured to diffuse in vain.

For, the people who were shovelling away on the house-tops were jovial and full of glee; calling out to one another from the parapets, and now and then exchanging a facetious snowball— better-natured missile far than many a wordy jest—laughing heartily if it went right and not less heartily if it went wrong. The poulterers' shops were still half open, and the fruiterers' were radiant in their glory. There were great, round, pot-bellied baskets of chestnuts, shaped like the waistcoats of jolly old gentlemen, lolling at the doors, and tumbling out into the street in their apoplectic opulence. There were ruddy, brown-faced, broad-girthed Spanish

Onions, shining in the fatness of their growth like Spanish Friars; and winking from their shelves in wanton slyness at the girls as they went by, and glanced demurely at the hung-up mistletoe. There were pears and apples, clustered high in blooming pyramids; there were bunches of grapes, made, in the shopkeepers' benevolence, to dangle from conspicuous hooks, that people's mouths might water gratis as they passed; there were piles of filberts, mossy and brown, recalling, in their fragrance, ancient walks among the woods, and pleasant shufflings ankle deep through withered leaves; there were Norfolk Biffins, squab and swarthy, setting off the yellow of the oranges and lemons, and, in the great compactness of their juicy persons, urgently entreating and beseeching to be carried home in paper bags and eaten after dinner. The very gold and silver fish, set forth among these choice fruits in a bowl, though members of a dull and stagnant-blooded race, appeared to know that there was something going on; and, to a fish, went gasping round and round their little world in slow and passionless excitement.

The Grocer's! oh the Grocer's! nearly closed, with perhaps two shutters down, or one; but through those gaps such glimpses! It was not alone that the scales descending on the counter made a merry sound, or that the twine and roller parted company so briskly, or that the canisters were rattled up and down like juggling tricks, or even that the blended scents of tea and coffee were so grateful to the nose, or even that the raisins were so plentiful and rare, the almonds so extremely white, the sticks of cinnamon so long and straight, the other spices so delicious, the candied fruits so caked and spotted with molten sugar as to make the coldest lookers-on feel faint and subsequently bilious. Nor was it that the figs were moist and pulpy, or that the French plums blushed in modest tartness from their highly decorated boxes, or that everything was good to eat and in its Christmas dress: but the customers were all so hurried and so eager in the hopeful promise of the day, that they tumbled up against each other at the door, clashing their wicker-baskets wildly, and left their purchases upon the counter, and came running back to fetch them, and committed hundreds of the like mistakes in the best humour possible; while the Grocer and his people were so frank and fresh that the polished hearts with which they fastened their aprons behind might have been their own, worn outside for general inspection, and for Christmas daws to peck at if they chose.

But soon the steeples called good people all,

to church and chapel, and away they came, flocking through the streets in their best clothes, and with their gayest faces. And at the same time there emerged from scores of bye-streets, lanes, and nameless turnings, innumerable people, carrying their dinners to the bakers' shops. The sight of these poor revellers appeared to interest the Spirit very much, for he stood with Scrooge beside him in a baker's doorway, and taking off the covers as their bearers passed, sprinkled incense on their dinners from his torch. And it was a very uncommon kind of torch, for once or twice when there were angry words between some dinner-carriers who had jostled with each other, he shed a few drops of water on them from it, and their good humour was restored directly. For they said, it was a shame to quarrel upon Christmas Day. And so it was! God love it, so it was!

In time the bells ceased, and the bakers were shut up; and yet there was a genial shadowing forth of all these dinners and the progress of their cooking, in the thawed blotch of wet above each baker's oven; where the pavement smoked as if its stones were cooking too.

" Is there a peculiar flavour in what you sprinkle from your torch? " asked Scrooge.

" There is. My own."

"Would it apply to any kind of dinner on this day?" asked Scrooge.

"To any kindly given. To a poor one most."

"Why to a poor one most?" asked Scrooge.

"Because it needs it most."

"Spirit," said Scrooge, after a moment's thought, "I wonder you, of all the beings in the many worlds about us, should desire to cramp these people's opportunities of innocent enjoyment."

"I!" cried the Spirit.

"You would deprive them of their means of dining every seventh day, often the only day on which they can be said to dine at all," said Scrooge. "Wouldn't you?"

"I!" cried the Spirit.

"You seek to close these places on the Seventh Day?" said Scrooge. "And it comes to the same thing."

"*I* seek!" exclaimed the Spirit.

"Forgive me if I am wrong. It has been done in your name, or at least in that of your family," said Scrooge.

"There are some upon this earth of yours," returned the Spirit, "who lay claim to know us, and who do their deeds of passion, pride, ill-will, hatred, envy, bigotry, and selfishness in our name, who are as strange to us and all our kith and kin, as if they had never lived. Remember that, and charge their doings on themselves, not us."

Scrooge promised that he would; and they went on, invisible, as they had been before, into the suburbs of the town. It was a remarkable quality of the Ghost (which Scrooge had observed at the baker's) that notwithstanding his gigantic size, he could accommodate himself to any place with ease; and that he stood beneath a low roof quite as gracefully and like a supernatural creature, as it was possible he could have done in any lofty hall.

And perhaps it was the pleasure the good Spirit had in showing off this power of his, or else it was his own kind, generous, hearty nature, and his sympathy with all poor men, that led him straight to Scrooge's clerk; for there he went, and took Scrooge with him, holding to his robe; and on the threshold of the door the Spirit smiled, and stopped to bless Bob Cratchit's dwelling with the sprinklings of his torch. Think of that! Bob had but fifteen " Bob " a-week himself; he pocketed on Saturdays but fifteen copies of his Christian name; and yet the Ghost of Christmas Present blessed his four-roomed house!

Then up rose Mrs. Cratchit, Cratchit's wife, dressed out but poorly in a twice-turned gown, but brave in ribbons, which are cheap and make a goodly show for sixpence; and she laid the cloth, assisted by Belinda Cratchit, second of her daughters, also brave in ribbons; while Master Peter Cratchit plunged a fork into the saucepan of potatoes, and getting the corners of his monstrous shirt collar (Bob's private property, conferred upon his son and heir in honour of the day) into his mouth, rejoiced to find himself so gallantly attired, and yearned to show his linen in the fashionable Parks. And now two smaller Cratchits, boy and girl, came tearing in, screaming that outside the baker's they had smelt the goose, and known it for their own; and basking in luxurious thoughts of sage-and-onion, these young Cratchits danced about the table, and exalted Master Peter Cratchit to the skies, while he (not proud, although his collars nearly choked him) blew the fire, until the slow potatoes bubbling up, knocked loudly at the saucepan-lid to be let out and peeled.

"What has ever got your precious father then?" said Mrs. Cratchit. "And your brother, Tiny Tim! And Martha warn't as late last Christmas Day by half-an-hour!"

"Here's Martha, mother!" said a girl, appearing as she spoke.

"Here's Martha, mother!" cried the two

young Cratchits. "Hurrah! There's *such* a goose, Martha!"

"Why, bless your heart alive, my dear, how late you are!" said Mrs. Cratchit, kissing her a dozen times, and taking off her shawl and bonnet for her with officious zeal.

"We'd a deal of work to finish up last night," replied the girl, "and had to clear away this morning, mother!"

"Well! Never mind so long as you are come," said Mrs. Cratchit. "Sit ye down before the fire, my dear, and have a warm, Lord bless ye!"

"No, no! There's father coming," cried the two young Cratchits, who were everywhere at once. "Hide, Martha, hide!"

So Martha hid herself, and in came little Bob, the father, with at least three feet of comforter exclusive of the fringe, hanging down before him; and his threadbare clothes darned up and brushed, to look seasonable; and Tiny Tim upon his shoulder. Alas for Tiny Tim, he bore a little crutch, and had his limbs supported by an iron frame!

"Why, where's our Martha?" cried Bob Cratchit, looking round.

"Not coming," said Mrs. Cratchit.

"Not coming!" said Bob, with a sudden declension in his high spirits; for he had been

Tim's blood horse all the way from church, and had come home rampant. " Not coming upon Christmas Day! "

Martha didn't like to see him disappointed, if it were only in joke; so she came out prematurely from behind the closet door, and ran into his arms, while the two young Cratchits hustled Tiny Tim, and bore him off into the wash-house, that he might hear the pudding singing in the copper.

" And how did little Tim behave? " asked Mrs. Cratchit, when she had rallied Bob on his credulity, and Bob had hugged his daughter to his heart's content.

" As good as gold," said Bob, " and better. Somehow he gets thoughtful, sitting by himself so much, and thinks the strangest things you ever heard. He told me, coming home, that he hoped the people saw him in the church, because he was a cripple, and it might be pleasant to them to remember upon Christmas Day, who made lame beggars walk and blind men see."

Bob's voice was tremulous when he told them this, and trembled more when he said that Tiny Tim was growing strong and hearty.

His active little crutch was heard upon the floor, and back came Tiny Tim before another word was spoken, escorted by his brother and sister to his stool before the fire; and while Bob, turning up his cuffs—as if, poor fellow, they were capable of being made more shabby — compounded some hot mixture in a jug with gin and lemons, and stirred it round and round and put it on the hob to simmer; Master Peter and the two ubiquitous young Cratchits went to fetch the goose, with which they soon returned in high procession.

Such a bustle ensued that you might have thought a goose the rarest of all birds; a feathered phenomenon, to which a black swan was a matter of course—and in truth it was something very like it in that house. Mrs. Cratchit made the gravy (ready beforehand in a little saucepan) hissing hot; Master Peter mashed the potatoes with incredible vigour; Miss Belinda sweetened up the apple-sauce; Martha dusted the hot plates; Bob took Tiny Tim beside him in a tiny corner at the table; the two young Cratchits set chairs for everybody, not forgetting themselves, and mounting guard upon their posts, crammed spoons into their mouths, lest they should shriek for goose before their turn came to be helped. At last the dishes were set on, and grace was said. It was succeeded by a breathless pause, as Mrs. Cratchit, looking slowly all along the carving-knife, prepared to plunge it in the breast; but when she did, and when the long-expected gush of stuffing issued forth, one murmur of delight arose all round the board, and even Tiny Tim, excited by the two young Cratchits, beat on the table with the handle of his knife, and feebly cried Hurrah!

There never was such a goose. Bob said he didn't believe there ever was such a goose cooked. Its tenderness and flavour, size and cheapness, were the themes of universal admiration. Eked out by the apple-sauce and mashed potatoes, it was a sufficient dinner for the whole family; indeed, as Mrs. Cratchit said with great delight (surveying one small atom of a bone upon the dish), they hadn't ate it all at last! Yet every one had had enough, and the youngest Cratchits in particular, were steeped in sage and onion to the eyebrows! But now, the plates being changed by Miss Belinda, Mrs. Cratchit left the room alone —too nervous to bear witnesses—to take the pudding up and bring it in.

Suppose it should not be done enough! Suppose it should break in turning out! Suppose somebody should have got over the wall of the back-yard, and stolen it, while they were merry with the goose—a supposition at which the two young Cratchits became livid! All sorts of horrors were supposed.

Halloa! A great deal of steam! The pudding

was out of the copper. A smell like a washing-day! That was the cloth. A smell like an eating-house and a pastry-cook's next door to each other, with a laundress's next door to that! That was the pudding! In half a minute Mrs. Cratchit entered—flushed, but smiling proudly—with the pudding, like a speckled cannon-ball, so hard and firm, blazing in half of half-a-quartern of ignited brandy, and bedight with Christmas holly stuck into the top.

Oh, a wonderful pudding! Bob Cratchit said, and calmly too, that he regarded it as the greatest success achieved by Mrs. Cratchit since their marriage. Mrs. Cratchit said that now the weight was off her mind, she would confess she had had her doubts about the quantity of flour. Everybody had something to say about it, but nobody said or thought it was at all a small pudding for a large family. It would have been flat heresy to do so. Any Cratchit would have blushed to hint at such a thing.

At last the dinner was all done, the cloth was cleared, the hearth swept, and the fire made up. The compound in the jug being tasted, and con-sidered perfect, apples and oranges were put upon the table, and a shovel-full of chestnuts on the fire. Then all the Cratchit family drew round the hearth, in what Bob Cratchit called a circle, meaning half a one; and at Bob Cratchit's elbow stood the family display of glass. Two tumblers, and a custard-cup without a handle.

These held the hot stuff from the jug, however, as well as golden goblets would have done; and Bob served it out with beaming looks, while the chestnuts on the fire sputtered and cracked noisily. Then Bob proposed:

" A merry Christmas to us all, my dears. God bless us! "

Which all the family re-echoed.

" God bless us every one! " said Tiny Tim, the last of all.

He sat very close to his father's side upon his little stool. Bob held his withered little hand in his, as if he loved the child, and wished to keep him by his side, and dreaded that he might be taken from him.

" Spirit," said Scrooge, with an interest he had never felt before, " tell me if Tiny Tim will live."

" I see a vacant seat," replied the Ghost, " in the poor chimney-corner, and a crutch without an owner, carefully preserved. If these shadows remain unaltered by the Future, the child will die."

" No, no," said Scrooge. " Oh no, kind Spirit! say he will be spared."

" If these shadows remain unaltered by the Future, none other of my race," returned the Ghost, " will find him here. What then? If he be like to die, he had better do it, and decrease the surplus population."

Scrooge hung his head to hear his own words quoted by the Spirit, and was overcome with penitence and grief.

" Man," said the Ghost, " if man you be in heart, not adamant, forbear that wicked cant until you have discovered What the surplus is, and Where it is. Will you decide what men shall live, what men shall die? It may be, that in the sight of Heaven, you are more worthless and less fit to live than millions like this poor man's child. Oh God! to hear the Insect on the leaf pronouncing on the too much life among his hungry brothers in the dust!"

Scrooge bent before the Ghost's rebuke, and trembling cast his eyes upon the ground. But he raised them speedily, on hearing his own name.

" Mr. Scrooge!" said Bob; " I'll give you Mr. Scrooge, the Founder of the Feast!"

" The Founder of the Feast indeed!" cried Mrs. Cratchit, reddening. " I wish I had him here. I'd give him a piece of my mind to feast upon, and I hope he'd have a good appetite for it."

" My dear," said Bob, " the children! Christmas Day."

" It should be Christmas Day, I am sure," said she, " on which one drinks the health of such an odious, stingy, hard, unfeeling man as Mr. Scrooge. You know he is, Robert! Nobody knows it better than you do, poor fellow! "

" My dear," was Bob's mild answer, " Christmas Day."

" I'll drink his health for your sake and the Day's," said Mrs. Cratchit, " not for his. Long life to him! A Merry Christmas and a Happy New Year! He'll be very merry and very happy, I have no doubt! "

The children drank the toast after her. It was the first of their proceedings which had no heartiness in it. Tiny Tim drank it last of all, but he didn't care twopence for it. Scrooge was the Ogre of the family. The mention of his name cast a dark shadow on the party, which was not dispelled for full five minutes.

After it had passed away, they were ten times merrier than before, from the mere relief of Scrooge the Baleful being done with. Bob Cratchit told them how he had a situation in his eye for Master Peter, which would bring in, if obtained, full five-and-sixpence weekly. The two young Cratchits laughed tremendously at

the idea of Peter's being a man of business; and
Peter himself looked thoughtfully at the fire from
between his collars, as if he were deliberating
what particular investments he should favour
when he came into the receipt of that bewilder-
ing income. Martha, who was a poor apprentice
at a milliner's, then told them what kind of
work she had to do, and how many hours she
worked at a stretch, and how she meant to lie
abed to-morrow morning for a good long rest;
to-morrow being a holiday she passed at home.
Also how she had seen a countess and a lord
some days before, and how the lord " was much
about as tall as Peter "; at which Peter pulled
up his collars so high that you couldn't have seen
his head if you had been there. All this time the
chestnuts and the jug went round and round;
and by-and-by they had a song, about a lost
child travelling in the snow, from Tiny Tim, who
had a plaintive little voice, and sang it very well
indeed.

There was nothing of high mark in this. They
were not a handsome family; they were not well
dressed; their shoes were far from being water-
proof; their clothes were scanty; and Peter
might have known, and very likely did, the inside of a pawnbroker's. But, they were happy,
grateful, pleased with one another, and contented

with the time; and when they faded, and looked happier yet in the bright sprinklings of the Spirit's torch at parting, Scrooge had his eye upon them, and especially on Tiny Tim, until the last.

By this time it was getting dark, and snowing pretty heavily; and as Scrooge and the Spirit went along the streets, the brightness of the roaring fires in kitchens, parlours, and all sorts of rooms, was wonderful. Here, the flickering of the blaze showed preparations for a cosy dinner, with hot plates baking through and through before the fire, and deep red curtains, ready to be drawn to shut out cold and darkness. There, all the children of the house were running out into the snow to meet their married sisters, brothers, cousins, uncles, aunts, and be the first to greet them. Here, again, were shadows on the window-blind of guests assembling; and there a group of handsome girls, all hooded and fur-booted, and all chattering at once, tripped lightly off to some near neighbour's house; where, woe upon the single man who saw them enter—artful witches: well they knew it—in a glow!

But if you had judged from the numbers of people on their way to friendly gatherings, you might have thought that no one was at home to give them welcome when they got there, instead of every house expecting company, and piling up its fires half-chimney high. Blessings on it, how the Ghost exulted! How it bared its breadth of breast, and opened its capacious palm, and floated on, outpouring, with a generous hand, its bright and harmless mirth on everything within its reach! The very lamplighter, who ran on before dotting the dusky street with specks of light, and who was dressed to spend the evening somewhere, laughed out loudly as the Spirit passed: though little kenned the lamplighter that he had any company but Christmas!

And now, without a word of warning from the Ghost, they stood upon a bleak and desert moor, where monstrous masses of rude stone were cast about, as though it were the burial-place of giants; and water spread itself wheresoever it listed, or would have done so, but for the frost that held it prisoner; and nothing grew but moss and furze, and coarse, rank grass. Down in the west the setting sun had left a streak of fiery red, which glared upon the desolation for an instant, like a sullen eye, and frowning lower, lower, lower yet, was lost in the thick gloom of darkest night.

" What place is this? " asked Scrooge.

" A place where Miners live, who labour in

the bowels of the earth," returned the Spirit. " But they know me. See! "

A light shone from the window of a hut, and swiftly they advanced towards it. Passing through the wall of mud and stone, they found a cheerful company assembled round a glowing fire. An old, old man and woman, with their children and their children's children, and another generation beyond that, all decked out gaily in their holiday attire. The old man, in a voice that seldom rose above the howling of the wind upon the barren waste, was singing them a Christmas song; it had been a very old song when he was a boy; and from time to time they all joined in the chorus. So surely as they raised their voices, the old man got quite blithe and loud; and so surely as they stopped, his vigour sank again.

The Spirit did not tarry here, but bade Scrooge hold his robe, and passing on above the moor, sped whither? Not to sea? To sea. To Scrooge's horror, looking back, he saw the last of the land, a frightful range of rocks, behind them; and his ears were deafened by the thundering of water, as it rolled, and roared, and raged among the dreadful caverns it had worn, and fiercely tried to undermine the earth.

Built upon a dismal reef of sunken rocks,

some league or so from shore, on which the waters chafed and dashed, the wild year through, there stood a solitary lighthouse. Great heaps of sea-weed clung to its base, and storm-birds—born of the wind one might suppose, as sea-weed of the water—rose and fell about it, like the waves they skimmed.

But even here, two men who watched the light had made a fire, that through the loop-hole in the thick stone wall shed out a ray of brightness on the awful sea. Joining their horny hands over the rough table at which they sat, they wished each other Merry Christmas in their can of grog; and one of them: the elder, too, with his face all damaged and scarred with hard weather, as the figure-head of an old ship might be: struck up a sturdy song that was like a Gale in itself.

Again the Ghost sped on, above the black and heaving sea—on, on—until, being far away, as he told Scrooge, from any shore, they lighted on a ship. They stood beside the helmsman at the wheel, the look-out in the bow, the officers who had the watch; dark, ghostly figures in their several stations; but every man among them hummed a Christmas tune, or had a Christmas thought, or spoke below his breath to his companion of some bygone Christmas Day, with homeward hopes belonging to it. And every man on board, waking or sleeping, good or bad, had had a kinder word for another on that day than on any day in the year; and had shared to some extent in its festivities; and had remembered those he cared for at a distance, and had known that they delighted to remember him.

It was a great surprise to Scrooge, while listening to the moaning of the wind, and thinking what a solemn thing it was to move on through the lonely darkness over an unknown abyss, whose depths were secrets as profound as Death: it was a great surprise to Scrooge, while thus engaged, to hear a hearty laugh. It was a much greater surprise to Scrooge to recognise it as his own nephew's and to find himself in a bright, dry, gleaming room, with the Spirit standing smiling by his side, and looking at that same nephew with approving affability.

" Ha, ha! " laughed Scrooge's nephew. " Ha, ha, ha! "

If you should happen, by any unlikely chance, to know a man more blest in a laugh than Scrooge's nephew, all I can say is, I should like to know him too. Introduce him to me, and I'll cultivate his acquaintance.

It is a fair, even-handed, noble adjustment of

D

things, that while there is infection in disease
and sorrow, there is nothing in the world so
irresistibly contagious as laughter and good-
humour. When Scrooge's nephew laughed in
this way: holding his sides, rolling his head,
and twisting his face into the most extrava-
gant contortions: Scrooge's niece, by marriage,
laughed as heartily as he. And their assembled
friends being not a bit behindhand, roared out
lustily.

" Ha, ha! Ha, ha, ha, ha! "

" He said that Christmas was a humbug, as
I live! " cried Scrooge's nephew. " He believed
it too! "

" More shame for him, Fred! " said Scrooge's
niece, indignantly. Bless those women; they
never do anything by halves. They are always
in earnest.

She was very pretty: exceedingly pretty.
With a dimpled, surprised-looking, capital face;
a ripe little mouth, that seemed made to be
kissed—as no doubt it was; all kinds of good
little dots about her chin, that melted into one
another when she laughed; and the sunniest pair
of eyes you ever saw in any little creature's head.
Altogether she was what you would have called
provoking, you know; but satisfactory, too.
Oh, perfectly satisfactory!

"He's a comical old fellow," said Scrooge's nephew, "that's the truth; and not so pleasant as he might be. However, his offences carry their own punishment, and I have nothing to say against him."

"I'm sure he is very rich, Fred," hinted Scrooge's niece. "At least you always tell *me* so."

"What of that, my dear!" said Scrooge's nephew. "His wealth is of no use to him. He don't do any good with it. He don't make himself comfortable with it. He hasn't the satisfaction of thinking—ha, ha, ha!—that he is ever going to benefit Us with it."

"I have no patience with him," observed Scrooge's niece. Scrooge's niece's sisters, and all the other ladies, expressed the same opinion.

"Oh, I have!" said Scrooge's nephew. "I am sorry for him; I couldn't be angry with him if I tried. Who suffers by his ill whims? Himself, always. Here, he takes it into his head to dislike us, and he won't come and dine with us. What's the consequence? He don't lose much of a dinner."

"Indeed, I think he loses a very good dinner," interrupted Scrooge's niece. Everybody else said the same, and they must be allowed to have been competent judges, because they had just had dinner; and, with the dessert upon the table, were clustered round the fire, by lamplight.

" Well! I'm very glad to hear it," said Scrooge's nephew, " because I haven't any great faith in these young housekeepers. What do *you* say, Topper? "

Topper had clearly got his eye upon one of Scrooge's niece's sisters, for he answered that a bachelor was a wretched outcast, who had no right to express an opinion on the subject. Whereat Scrooge's niece's sister—the plump one with the lace tucker: not the one with the roses—blushed.

" Do go on, Fred," said Scrooge's niece, clapping her hands. " He never finishes what he begins to say! He is such a ridiculous fellow! "

Scrooge's nephew revelled in another laugh, and as it was impossible to keep the infection off; though the plump sister tried hard to do it with aromatic vinegar; his example was unanimously followed.

" I was only going to say," said Scrooge's nephew, " that the consequence of his taking a dislike to us, and not making merry with us, is, as I think, that he loses some pleasant moments, which could do him no harm. I am sure he loses pleasanter companions than he can find in his own thoughts, either in his mouldy old office, or his dusty chambers. I mean to give him the same chance every year, whether he likes it or not, for I pity him. He may rail at Christmas till he dies, but he can't help thinking better of it—I defy him—if he finds me going there, in good temper, year after year, and saying 'Uncle Scrooge, how are you?' If it only puts him in the vein to leave his poor clerk fifty pounds, *that's* something; and I think I shook him yesterday."

It was their turn to laugh now at the notion of his shaking Scrooge. But being thoroughly good-natured, and not much caring what they laughed at, so that they laughed at any rate, he encouraged them in their merriment, and passed the bottle joyously.

After tea, they had some music. For they were a musical family, and knew what they were about, when they sang a Glee or Catch, I can assure you: especially Topper, who could growl away in the bass like a good one, and never swell the large veins in his forehead, or get red in the face over it. Scrooge's niece played well upon the harp; and played among other tunes a simple little air (a mere nothing: you might learn to whistle it in two minutes), which had been familiar to the child who fetched Scrooge from the boarding-school, as he had been reminded by the Ghost of Christmas Past. When this strain of music sounded, all the things that Ghost had shown him, came upon his mind; he softened more and more; and thought that if he could have listened to it often, years ago, he might have cultivated the kindnesses of life for his own happiness with his own hands, without resorting to the sexton's spade that buried Jacob Marley.

But they didn't devote the whole evening to music. After a while they played at forfeits; for it is good to be children sometimes, and never better than at Christmas, when its mighty Founder was a child himself. Stop! There was first a game at blindman's-buff. Of course there was. And I no more believe Topper was really blind than I believe he had eyes in his boots. My opinion is, that it was a done thing between him and Scrooge's nephew: and that the Ghost of Christmas Present knew it. The way he went after that plump sister in the lace tucker, was an outrage on the credulity of human nature. Knocking down the fire-irons, tumbling over the chairs, bumping up against the piano, smothering himself among the curtains, wherever she went, there went he. He always knew where the plump sister was. He wouldn't catch anybody else. If you had fallen up against him, as some of them

A corner whence there was no escape

C.E.Brock 1905

did, and stood there, he would have made a
feint of endeavouring to seize you, which would
have been an affront to your understanding;
and would instantly have sidled off in the direction of the plump sister. She often cried out that
it wasn't fair; and it really was not. But when,
at last, he caught her; when, in spite of all her
silken rustlings, and her rapid flutterings past

him, he got her into a corner whence there was no
escape; then his conduct was the most execrable.
For his pretending not to know her; his pretending that it was necessary to touch her head-dress,
and further to assure himself of her identity by
pressing a certain ring upon her finger, and a
certain chain about her neck; was vile, monstrous! No doubt she told him her opinion of it,
when, another blind man being in office, they
were so very confidential together, behind the
curtains.

Scrooge's niece was not one of the blindman's-
buff party, but was made comfortable with a
large chair and a footstool, in a snug corner,
where the Ghost and Scrooge were close behind
her. But she joined in the forfeits, and loved her
love to admiration with all the letters of the
alphabet. Likewise at the game of How, When,
and Where, she was very great, and to the secret
joy of Scrooge's nephew, beat her sisters hollow:
though they were sharp girls too, as Topper could
have told you. There might have been twenty
people there, young and old, but they all played,
and so did Scrooge; for, wholly forgetting in
the interest he had in what was going on, that
his voice made no sound in their ears, he sometimes came out with his guess quite loud, and
very often guessed quite right, too; for the

sharpest needle, best Whitechapel, warranted not
to cut in the eye, was not sharper than Scrooge;
blunt as he took it in his head to be.

The Ghost was greatly pleased to find him in
this mood, and looked upon him with such favour,
that he begged like a boy to be allowed to stay
until the guests departed. But this the Spirit
said could not be done.

"Here is a new game," said Scrooge. "One
half-hour, Spirit, only one."

It is a game called Yes and No, where Scrooge's
nephew had to think of something, and the rest
must find out what; he only answering to their
questions yes or no, as the case was. The brisk
fire of questioning to which he was exposed,
elicited from him that he was thinking of an
animal, a live animal, rather a disagreeable
animal, a savage animal, an animal that growled
and grunted sometimes, and talked sometimes,
and lived in London, and walked about the
streets, and wasn't made a show of, and wasn't
led by anybody, and didn't live in a menagerie,
and was never killed in a market, and was not
a horse, or an ass, or a cow, or a bull, or a tiger,
or a dog, or a pig, or a cat, or a bear. At every
fresh question that was put to him, this nephew
burst into a fresh roar of laughter; and was so
inexpressibly tickled, that he was obliged to get

*D

off the sofa and stamp. At last the plump sister, falling into a similar state, cried out:

"I have found it out! I know what it is, Fred! I know what it is!"

"What is it?" cried Fred.

"It's your Uncle Scro-o-o-o-oge!"

Which it certainly was. Admiration was the universal sentiment, though some objected that the reply to "Is it a bear?" ought to have been "Yes"; inasmuch as an answer in the negative was sufficient to have diverted their thoughts from Mr. Scrooge, supposing they had ever had any tendency that way.

"He has given us plenty of merriment, I am sure," said Fred, "and it would be ungrateful not to drink his health. Here is a glass of mulled wine ready to our hand at the moment; and I say, 'Uncle Scrooge!'"

"Well! Uncle Scrooge!" they cried.

"A Merry Christmas and a Happy New Year to the old man, whatever he is!" said Scrooge's nephew. "He wouldn't take it from me, but may he have it, nevertheless. Uncle Scrooge!"

Uncle Scrooge had imperceptibly become so gay and light of heart, that he would have pledged the unconscious company in return, and thanked them in an inaudible speech, if the Ghost had given him time. But the whole scene passed off in the breath of the last word spoken by his nephew; and he and the Spirit were again upon their travels.

Much they saw, and far they went, and many homes they visited, but always with a happy end. The Spirit stood beside sick-beds, and they were cheerful; on foreign lands, and they were close at home; by struggling men, and they were patient in their greater hope; by poverty, and it was rich. In almshouse, hospital, and jail, in misery's every refuge, where vain man in his little brief authority had not made fast the door, and barred the Spirit out, he left his blessing, and taught Scrooge his precepts.

It was a long night, if it were only a night; but Scrooge had his doubts of this, because the Christmas Holidays appeared to be condensed into the space of time they passed together. It was strange, too, that while Scrooge remained unaltered in his outward form, the Ghost grew older, clearly older. Scrooge had observed this change, but never spoke of it, until they left a children's Twelfth Night party, when, looking at the Spirit as they stood together in an open place, he noticed that its hair was grey.

" Are spirits' lives so short? " asked Scrooge.

" My life upon this globe is very brief," replied the Ghost. " It ends to-night."

"To-night!" cried Scrooge.

"To-night at midnight. Hark! The time is drawing near."

The chimes were ringing the three quarters past eleven at that moment.

"Forgive me if I am not justified in what I ask," said Scrooge, looking intently at the Spirit's robe, "but I see something strange, and not belonging to yourself, protruding from your skirts. Is it a foot or a claw?"

"It might be a claw, for the flesh there is upon it," was the Spirit's sorrowful reply. "Look here."

From the folds of its robe, it brought two children; wretched, abject, frightful, hideous, miserable. They knelt down at its feet, and clung upon the outside of its garment.

"Oh, Man! look here. Look, look, down here!" exclaimed the Ghost.

They were a boy and girl. Yellow, meagre, ragged, scowling, wolfish; but prostrate, too, in their humility. Where graceful youth should have filled their features out, and touched them with its freshest tints, a stale and shrivelled hand, like that of age, had pinched, and twisted them, and pulled them into shreds. Where angels might have sat enthroned, devils lurked, and glared out menacing. No change, no degradation, no perversion of humanity, in any grade, through all the mysteries of wonderful creation, has monsters half so horrible and dread.

Scrooge started back, appalled. Having them shown to him in this way, he tried to say they were fine children, but the words choked themselves, rather than be parties to a lie of such enormous magnitude.

"Spirit! are they yours?" Scrooge could say no more.

"They are Man's," said the Spirit, looking down upon them. "And they cling to me, appealing from their fathers. This boy is Ignorance. This girl is Want. Beware them both, and all of their degree, but most of all beware this boy, for on his brow I see that written which is Doom, unless the writing be erased. Deny it!" cried the Spirit, stretching out its hand towards the city. "Slander those who tell it ye! Admit it for your factious purposes, and make it worse! And bide the end!"

"Have they no refuge or resource?" cried Scrooge.

"Are there no prisons?" said the Spirit, turning on him for the last time with his own words. "Are there no workhouses?"

The bell struck twelve.

Scrooge looked about him for the Ghost, and saw it not. As the last stroke ceased to vibrate, he remembered the prediction of old Jacob Marley, and lifting up his eyes, beheld a solemn Phantom, draped and hooded, coming, like a mist along the ground, towards him.

Stave Four
The last of the Spirits

"No" said a great fat man......
"I only know he's dead"

THE Phantom slowly, gravely, silently approached. When it came near him, Scrooge bent down upon his knee; for in the very air through which this Spirit moved it seemed to scatter gloom and mystery.

It was shrouded in a deep black garment, which concealed its head, its face, its form, and left nothing of it visible save one outstretched hand. But for this it would have been difficult to detach its figure from the night, and separate it from the darkness by which it was surrounded.

He felt that it was tall and stately when it came beside him, and that its mysterious presence filled him with a solemn dread. He knew no more, for the Spirit neither spoke nor moved.

" I am in the presence of the Ghost of Christmas Yet To Come? " said Scrooge.

The Spirit answered not, but pointed downward with its hand.

" You are about to show me shadows of the things that have not happened, but will happen in the time before us," Scrooge pursued. " Is that so, Spirit? "

The upper portion of the garment was contracted for an instant in its folds, as if the Spirit had inclined its head. That was the only answer he received.

Although well used to ghostly company by this time, Scrooge feared the silent shape so much that his legs trembled beneath him, and he found that he could hardly stand when he prepared to follow it. The Spirit paused a moment, as observing his condition, and giving him time to recover.

But Scrooge was all the worse for this. It thrilled him with a vague uncertain horror, to know that behind the dusky shroud there were ghostly eyes intently fixed upon him, while he, though he stretched his own to the utmost, could see nothing but a spectral hand, and one great heap of black.

"Ghost of the Future!" he exclaimed, "I fear you more than any Spectre I have seen. But, as I know your purpose is to do me good, and as I hope to live to be another man from what I was, I am prepared to bear you company, and do it with a thankful heart. Will you not speak to me?"

It gave him no reply. The hand was pointed straight before them.

"Lead on!" said Scrooge. "Lead on! The night is waning fast, and it is precious time to me, I know. Lead on, Spirit!"

The Phantom moved away as it had come towards him. Scrooge followed in the shadow of its dress, which bore him up, he thought, and carried him along.

They scarcely seemed to enter the City; for the City rather seemed to spring up about them, and encompass them of its own act. But there they were, in the heart of it; on 'Change, amongst the merchants; who hurried up and down, and chinked the money in their pockets, and conversed in groups, and looked at their watches, and trifled thoughtfully with their great gold seals; and so forth, as Scrooge had seen them often.

The Spirit stopped beside one little knot of business men. Observing that the hand was pointed to them, Scrooge advanced to listen to their talk.

" No," said a great fat man with a monstrous chin, " I don't know much about it, either way. I only know he's dead."

" When did he die? " inquired another.

" Last night, I believe."

" Why, what was the matter with him? " asked a third, taking a vast quantity of snuff out of a very large snuff-box. " I thought he'd never die."

" God knows," said the first, with a yawn.

" What has he done with his money? " asked a red-faced gentleman with a pendulous excrescence on the end of his nose, that shook like the gills of a turkey-cock.

" I haven't heard," said the man with the large chin, yawning again. " Left it to his Company, perhaps. He hasn't left it to *me*. That's all I know."

This pleasantry was received with a general laugh.

" It's likely to be a very cheap funeral," said the same speaker; " for upon my life I don't know of anybody to go to it. Suppose we make up a party and volunteer?"

"I don't mind going if a lunch is provided," observed the gentleman with the excrescence on his nose. "But I must be fed, if I make one."

Another laugh.

"Well, I am the most disinterested among you, after all," said the first speaker, "for I never wear black gloves, and I never eat lunch. But I'll offer to go, if anybody else will. When I come to think of it, I'm not at all sure that I wasn't his most particular friend; for we used to stop and speak whenever we met. Bye, bye!"

Speakers and listeners strolled away, and mixed with other groups. Scrooge knew the men, and looked towards the Spirit for an explanation.

The Phantom glided on into a street. Its finger pointed to two persons meeting. Scrooge listened again, thinking that the explanation might lie here.

He knew these men, also, perfectly. They were men of business: very wealthy, and of great importance. He had made a point always of standing well in their esteem: in a business point of view, that is; strictly in a business point of view.

"How are you?" said one.

" How are you? " returned the other.

" Well! " said the first. " Old Scratch has got his own at last, hey? "

" So I am told," returned the second. " Cold, isn't it? "

" Seasonable for Christmas time. You're not a skater, I suppose? "

" No. No. Something else to think of. Good morning! "

Not another word. That was their meeting, their conversation, and their parting.

Scrooge was at first inclined to be surprised that the Spirit should attach importance to conversations apparently so trivial; but feeling assured that they must have some hidden purpose, he set himself to consider what it was likely to be. They could scarcely be supposed to have any bearing on the death of Jacob, his old partner, for that was Past, and this Ghost's province was the Future. Nor could he think of any one immediately connected with himself, to whom he could apply them. But nothing doubting that to whomsoever they applied they had some latent moral for his own improvement, he resolved to treasure up every word he heard, and everything he saw; and especially to observe the shadow of himself when it appeared. For he had an expectation that the conduct of his future self would give him the clue he missed, and would render the solution of these riddles easy.

He looked about in that very place for his own image; but another man stood in his accustomed corner, and though the clock pointed to his usual time of day for being there, he saw no likeness of himself among the multitudes that poured in through the Porch. It gave him little surprise, however; for he had been revolving in his mind a change of life, and thought and hoped he saw his new-born resolutions carried out in this.

Quiet and dark, beside him stood the Phantom, with its outstretched hand. When he roused himself from his thoughtful quest, he fancied from the turn of the hand, and its situation in reference to himself, that the Unseen Eyes were looking at him keenly. It made him shudder, and feel very cold.

They left the busy scene, and went into an obscure part of the town, where Scrooge had never penetrated before, although he recognised its situation, and its bad repute. The ways were foul and narrow; the shops and houses wretched; the people half-naked, drunken, slipshod, ugly. Alleys and archways, like so many cesspools, disgorged their offences of smell, and dirt, and life, upon the straggling streets; and the whole quarter reeked with crime, with filth, and misery.

Far in this den of infamous resort, there was a low-browed, beetling shop, below a pent-house roof, where iron, old rags, bottles, bones, and greasy offal, were bought. Upon the floor within, were piled up heaps of rusty keys, nails, chains, hinges, files, scales, weights, and refuse iron of all kinds. Secrets that few would like to scrutinise were bred and hidden in mountains of unseemly rags, masses of corrupted fat, and sepulchres of bones. Sitting in among the wares he dealt in, by a charcoal-stove, made of old bricks, was a grey-haired rascal, nearly seventy years of age; who had screened himself from the cold air without, by a frousy curtaining of miscellaneous tatters, hung upon a line ; and smoked his pipe in all the luxury of calm retirement.

Scrooge and the Phantom came into the presence of this man, just as a woman with a heavy bundle slunk into the shop. But she had scarcely entered, when another woman, similarly laden, came in too; and she was closely followed by a man in faded black, who was no less startled by the sight of them, than they had been upon the recognition of each other. After a short period

of blank astonishment, in which the old man
with the pipe had joined them, they all three
burst into a laugh.

" Let the charwoman alone to be the first! "
cried she who had entered first. " Let the laundress alone to be the second; and let the undertaker's man alone to be the third. Look here,
old Joe, here's a chance! If we haven't all three
met here without meaning it! "

" You couldn't have met in a better place,"
said old Joe, removing his pipe from his mouth.
" Come into the parlour. You were made free
of it long ago, you know; and the other two
an't strangers. Stop till I shut the door of the
shop. Ah! How it skreeks! There an't such a
rusty bit of metal in the place as its own hinges,
I believe; and I'm sure there's no such old bones
here as mine. Ha, ha! We're all suitable to our
calling, we're well matched. Come into the
parlour. Come into the parlour."

The parlour was the space behind the screen
of rags. The old man raked the fire together
with an old stair-rod, and having trimmed his
smoky lamp (for it was night) with the stem of
his pipe, put it in his mouth again.

While he did this, the woman who had already
spoken threw her bundle on the floor, and sat
down in a flaunting manner on a stool; crossing

her elbows on her knees, and looking with a bold defiance at the other two.

"What odds then! What odds, Mrs. Dilber?" said the woman. "Every person has a right to take care of themselves. *He* always did!"

"That's true, indeed!" said the laundress. "No man more so."

"Why, then, don't stand staring as if you was afraid, woman; who's the wiser? We're not going to pick holes in each other's coats, I suppose?"

"No, indeed!" said Mrs. Dilber and the man together. "We should hope not."

"Very well, then!" cried the woman. "That's enough. Who's the worse for the loss of a few things like these? Not a dead man, I suppose?"

"No, indeed," said Mrs. Dilber, laughing.

"If he wanted to keep 'em after he was dead, a wicked old screw," pursued the woman, "why wasn't he natural in his lifetime? If he had been, he'd have had somebody to look after him when he was struck with Death, instead of lying gasping out his last there, alone by himself."

"It's the truest word that ever was spoke," said Mrs. Dilber. "It's a judgment on him."

"I wish it was a little heavier one," replied the woman; "and it should have been, you may depend upon it, if I could have laid my hands on anything else. Open that bundle, old Joe, and let me know the value of it. Speak out plain. I'm not afraid to be the first, nor afraid for them to see it. We knew pretty well that we were helping ourselves, before we met here, I believe. It's no sin. Open the bundle, Joe."

But the gallantry of her friends would not allow of this; and the man in faded black, mounting the breach first, produced *his* plunder. It was not extensive. A seal or two, a pencil-case, a pair of sleeve-buttons, and a brooch of no great value, were all. They were severally examined and appraised by old Joe, who chalked the sums he was disposed to give for each, upon the wall, and added them up into a total when he found there was nothing more to come.

"That's your account," said Joe, "and I wouldn't give another sixpence, if I was to be boiled for not doing it. Who's next?"

Mrs. Dilber was next. Sheets and towels, a little wearing apparel, two old-fashioned silver teaspoons, a pair of sugar-tongs, and a few boots. Her account was stated on the wall in the same manner.

"I always give too much to ladies. It's a weakness of mine, and that's the way I ruin myself," said old Joe. "That's your account. If you asked me for another penny, and made it an open question, I'd repent of being so liberal and knock off half-a-crown."

"And now undo *my* bundle, Joe," said the first woman.

Joe went down on his knees for the greater convenience of opening it, and having unfastened a great many knots, dragged out a large and heavy roll of some dark stuff.

"What do you call this?" said Joe. "Bed-curtains!"

"Ah!" returned the woman, laughing and leaning forward on her crossed arms. "Bed-curtains!"

"You don't mean to say you took 'em down, rings and all, with him lying there?" said Joe.

"Yes I do," replied the woman. "Why not?"

"You were born to make your fortune," said Joe, "and you'll certainly do it."

"I certainly sha'n't hold my hand, when I can get anything in it by reaching it out, for the sake of such a man as He was, I promise you, Joe," returned the woman, coolly. "Don't drop that oil upon the blankets, now."

"His blankets?" asked Joe.

"Whose else's do you think?" replied the woman. "He isn't likely to take cold without 'em, I dare say."

What do you call this? said Joe

"I hope he didn't die of anything catching? Eh?" said old Joe, stopping in his work, and looking up.

"Don't you be afraid of that," returned the woman. "I an't so fond of his company that I'd loiter about him for such things, if he did. Ah!

you may look through that shirt till your eyes ache; but you won't find a hole in it, nor a threadbare place. It's the best he had, and a fine one too. They'd have wasted it, if it hadn't been for me."

"What do you call wasting of it?" asked old Joe.

"Putting it on him to be buried in, to be sure," replied the woman with a laugh. "Somebody was fool enough to do it, but I took it off again. If calico an't good enough for such a purpose, it isn't good enough for anything. It's quite as becoming to the body. He can't look uglier than he did in that one."

Scrooge listened to this dialogue in horror. As they sat grouped about their spoil, in the scanty light afforded by the old man's lamp, he viewed them with a detestation and disgust, which could hardly have been greater, though they had been obscene demons, marketing the corpse itself.

"Ha, ha!" laughed the same woman, when old Joe, producing a flannel bag with money in it, told out their several gains upon the ground. "This is the end of it, you see! He frightened every one away from him when he was alive, to profit us when he was dead! Ha, ha, ha!"

"Spirit!" said Scrooge, shuddering from head

to foot. " I see, I see. The case of this unhappy man might be my own. My life tends that way, now. Merciful Heaven, what is this! "

He recoiled in terror, for the scene had changed, and now he almost touched a bed: a bare, un-curtained bed: on which, beneath a ragged sheet, there lay a something covered up, which, though it was dumb, announced itself in awful language.

The room was very dark, too dark to be observed with any accuracy, though Scrooge glanced round it in obedience to a secret impulse, anxious to know what kind of room it was. A pale light, rising in the outer air, fell straight upon the bed; and on it, plundered and bereft, unwatched, unwept, uncared for, was the body of this man.

Scrooge glanced towards the Phantom. Its steady hand was pointed to the head. The cover was so carelessly adjusted that the slightest raising of it, the motion of a finger upon Scrooge's part, would have disclosed the face. He thought of it, felt how easy it would be to do, and longed to do it; but had no more power to withdraw the veil than to dismiss the spectre at his side.

Oh cold, cold, rigid, dreadful Death, set up thine altar here, and dress it with such terrors as thou hast at thy command: for this is thy dominion! But of the loved, revered, and honoured head, thou canst not turn one hair to thy dread purposes, or make one feature odious. It is not that the hand is heavy and will fall down when released; it is not that the heart and pulse are still; but that the hand WAS open, generous, and true; the heart brave, warm, and tender; and the pulse a man's. Strike, Shadow, strike! And see the good deeds springing from the wound, to sow the world with life immortal!

No voice pronounced these words in Scrooge's ears, and yet he heard them when he looked upon the bed. He thought, if this man could be raised up now, what would be his foremost thoughts? Avarice, hard dealing, griping cares? They have brought him to a rich end, truly!

He lay, in the dark empty house, with not a man, a woman, or a child, to say that he was kind to me in this or that, and for the memory of one kind word I will be kind to him. A cat was tearing at the door, and there was a sound of gnawing rats beneath the hearth-stone. What *they* wanted in the room of death, and why they were so restless and disturbed, Scrooge did not dare to think.

" Spirit! " he said, " this is a fearful place. In leaving it, I shall not leave its lesson, trust me. Let us go! "

Still the Ghost pointed with an unmoved finger to the head.

" I understand you," Scrooge returned, " and I would do it, if I could. But I have not the power, Spirit. I have not the power."

Again it seemed to look upon him.

" If there is any person in the town, who feels emotion caused by this man's death," said Scrooge, quite agonised, " show that person to me, Spirit, I beseech you! "

The Phantom spread its dark robe before him for a moment, like a wing; and withdrawing it, revealed a room by daylight, where a mother and her children were.

She was expecting some one, and with anxious eagerness; for she walked up and down the room; started at every sound; looked out from the window; glanced at the clock; tried, but in vain, to work with her needle; and could hardly bear the voices of the children in their play.

At length the long-expected knock was heard. She hurried to the door, and met her husband; a man whose face was careworn and depressed, though he was young. There was a remarkable expression in it now; a kind of serious delight of which he felt ashamed, and which he struggled to repress.

He sat down to the dinner that had been hoarding for him by the fire; and when she asked him faintly what news (which was not until after a long silence), he appeared embarrassed how to answer.

" Is it good," she said, " or bad? "—to help him.

" Bad," he answered.

" We are quite ruined? "

" No. There is hope yet, Caroline."

" If *he* relents," she said amazed, " there is! Nothing is past hope, if such a miracle has happened."

" He is past relenting," said her husband. " He is dead."

She was a mild and patient creature if her face spoke truth; but she was thankful in her soul to hear it, and she said so, with clasped hands. She prayed forgiveness the next moment, and was sorry; but the first was the emotion of her heart.

" What the half-drunken woman whom I told you of last night said to me, when I tried to see him and obtain a week's delay; and what I thought was a mere excuse to avoid me; turns out to have been quite true. He was not only very ill, but dying, then."

" To whom will our debt be transferred? "

" I don't know. But before that time we shall be ready with the money; and even though we

were not, it would be bad fortune indeed to find
so merciless a creditor in his successor. We may
sleep to-night with light hearts, Caroline!"

Yes.   Soften it as they would, their hearts
were lighter. The children's faces, hushed, and
clustered round to hear what they so little understood, were brighter; and it was a happier house
for this man's death! The only emotion that the
Ghost could show him, caused by the event, was
one of pleasure.

"Let me see some tenderness connected with
a death," said Scrooge; "or that dark chamber,
Spirit, which we left just now, will be for ever
present to me."

The Ghost conducted him through several
streets familiar to his feet; and as they went
along, Scrooge looked here and there to find himself, but nowhere was he to be seen. They entered
poor Bob Cratchit's house; the dwelling he had
visited before; and found the mother and the
children seated round the fire.

Quiet. Very quiet. The noisy little Cratchits
were as still as statues in one corner, and sat
looking up at Peter, who had a book before him.
The mother and her daughters were engaged in
sewing. But surely they were very quiet!

"'And He took a child, and set him in the
midst of them.'"

E

Where had Scrooge heard those words? He had not dreamed them. The boy must have read them out, as he and the Spirit crossed the threshold. Why did he not go on?

The mother laid her work upon the table, and put her hand up to her face.

"The colour hurts my eyes," she said.

The colour? Ah, poor Tiny Tim!

"They're better now again," said Cratchit's wife. "It makes them weak by candle-light; and I wouldn't show weak eyes to your father when he comes home, for the world. It must be near his time."

"Past it rather," Peter answered, shutting up his book. "But I think he's walked a little slower than he used, these few last evenings, mother."

They were very quiet again. At last she said, and in a steady cheerful voice, that only faltered once:

"I have known him walk with—I have known him walk with Tiny Tim upon his shoulder, very fast indeed."

"And so have I," cried Peter. "Often."

"And so have I," exclaimed another. So had all.

"But he was very light to carry," she resumed, intent upon her work, "and his father loved him so, that it was no trouble—no trouble. And there is your father at the door!"

She hurried out to meet him; and little Bob in his comforter—he had need of it, poor fellow —came in. His tea was ready for him on the hob, and they all tried who should help him to it most. Then the two young Cratchits got upon his knees and laid, each child a little cheek, against his face, as if they said, "Don't mind it, father. Don't be grieved!"

Bob was very cheerful with them, and spoke pleasantly to all the family. He looked at the work upon the table, and praised the industry and speed of Mrs. Cratchit and the girls. They would be done long before Sunday, he said.

"Sunday! You went to-day then, Robert?" said his wife.

"Yes, my dear," returned Bob. "I wish you could have gone. It would have done you good to see how green a place it is. But you'll see it often. I promised him that I would walk there on a Sunday. My little, little child!" cried Bob. "My little child!"

He broke down all at once. He couldn't help it. If he could have helped it, he and his child would have been farther apart perhaps than they were.

He left the room, and went up stairs into the

room above, which was lighted cheerfully, and
hung with Christmas. There was a chair set
close beside the child, and there were signs of
some one having been there, lately. Poor Bob
sat down in it, and when he had thought a little
and composed himself, he kissed the little face.
He was reconciled to what had happened, and
went down again quite happy.

They drew about the fire, and talked; the
girls and mother working still. Bob told them
of the extraordinary kindness of Mr. Scrooge's
nephew, whom he had scarcely seen but once,
and who, meeting him in the street that day,
and seeing that he looked a little—" just a little
down, you know," said Bob, inquired what had
happened to distress him. "On which," said
Bob, " for he is the pleasantest-spoken gentleman
you ever heard, I told him. ' I am heartily sorry
for it, Mr. Cratchit,' he said, ' and heartily sorry
for your good wife.' By the bye, how he ever
knew *that*, I don't know."

" Knew what, my dear? "

" Why, that you were a good wife," replied
Bob.

" Everybody knows that! " said Peter.

" Very well observed, my boy! " cried Bob.
" I hope they do. ' Heartily sorry,' he said, ' for
your good wife. If I can be of service to you in

any way,' he said, giving me his card, 'that's where I live. Pray come to me.' Now it wasn't," cried Bob, " for the sake of anything he might be able to do for us, so much as for his kind way, that this was quite delightful. It really seemed as if he had known our Tiny Tim, and felt with us."

" I'm sure he's a good soul! " said Mrs. Cratchit.

" You would be surer of it, my dear," returned Bob, " if you saw and spoke to him. I shouldn't be at all surprised, mark what I say, if he got Peter a better situation."

" Only hear that, Peter," said Mrs. Cratchit.

" And then," cried one of the girls, " Peter will be keeping company with some one, and setting up for himself."

" Get along with you! " retorted Peter, grinning.

" It's just as likely as not," said Bob, " one of these days; though there's plenty of time for that, my dear. But however and whenever we part from one another, I am sure we shall none of us forget poor Tiny Tim—shall we—or this first parting that there was among us? "

" Never, father! " cried they all.

" And I know," said Bob, " I know, my dears, that when we recollect how patient and how mild he was; although he was a little, little child; we shall not quarrel easily among ourselves, and forget poor Tiny Tim in doing it."

" No, never, father! " they all cried again.

" I am very happy," said little Bob, " I am very happy! "

Mrs. Cratchit kissed him, his daughters kissed him, the two young Cratchits kissed him, and Peter and himself shook hands. Spirit of Tiny Tim, thy childish essence was from God!

" Spectre," said Scrooge, " something informs me that our parting moment is at hand. I know it, but I know not how. Tell me what man that was whom we saw lying dead? "

The Ghost of Christmas Yet To Come conveyed him as before—though at a different time, he thought: indeed, there seemed no order in these latter visions, save that they were in the Future —into the resorts of business men, but showed him not himself. Indeed, the Spirit did not stay for anything, but went straight on, as to the end just now desired, until besought by Scrooge to tarry for a moment.

" This court," said Scrooge, " through which we hurry now, is where my place of occupation is, and has been for a length of time. I see the house. Let me behold what I shall be, in days to come! "

The Spirit stopped; the hand was pointed elsewhere.

"The house is yonder," Scrooge exclaimed.
"Why do you point away?"

The inexorable finger underwent no change.

Scrooge hastened to the window of his office,
and looked in. It was an office still, but not his.
The furniture was not the same, and the figure in
the chair was not himself. The Phantom pointed
as before.

He joined it once again, and wondering why
and whither he had gone, accompanied it until
they reached an iron gate. He paused to look
round before entering.

A churchyard. Here, then, the wretched man
whose name he had now to learn, lay underneath
the ground. It was a worthy place. Walled in by
houses; overrun by grass and weeds, the growth
of vegetation's death, not life; choked up with
too much burying; fat with repleted appetite.
A worthy place!

The Spirit stood among the graves, and pointed
down to One. He advanced towards it trembling.
The Phantom was exactly as it had been, but he
dreaded that he saw new meaning in its solemn
shape.

"Before I draw nearer to that stone to which
you point," said Scrooge, "answer me one question. Are these the shadows of things that Will be,
or are they shadows of things that May be, only?"

Still the Ghost pointed downward to the grave by which it stood.

" Men's courses will foreshadow certain ends, to which, if persevered in, they must lead," said Scrooge. " But if the courses be departed from, the ends will change. Say it is thus with what you show me! "

The Spirit was immovable as ever.

Scrooge crept towards it, trembling as he went; and following the finger, read upon the stone of the neglected grave his own name, EBENEZER SCROOGE.

" Am *I* that man who lay upon the bed? " he cried, upon his knees.

The finger pointed from the grave to him, and back again.

" No, Spirit! Oh no, no! "

The finger was still there.

" Spirit! " he cried, tight clutching at its robe, " hear me! I am not the man I was. I will not be the man I must have been but for this intercourse. Why show me this, if I am past all hope! "

For the first time the hand appeared to shake.

" Good Spirit," he pursued, as down upon the ground he fell before it: " Your nature intercedes for me, and pities me. Assure me that I yet may change these shadows you have shown me, by an altered life! "

The kind hand trembled.

" I will honour Christmas in my heart, and try to keep it all the year. I will live in the Past, the Present, and the Future. The Spirits of all Three shall strive within me. I will not shut out the lessons that they teach. Oh, tell me I may sponge away the writing on this stone! "

In his agony, he caught the spectral hand. It sought to free itself, but he was strong in his entreaty, and detained it. The Spirit, stronger yet, repulsed him.

Holding up his hands in one last prayer to have his fate reversed, he saw an alteration in the Phantom's hood and dress. It shrank, collapsed, and dwindled down into a bedpost.

*E

Stave Five
The end of it

It was a Turkey

YES! and the bedpost was his own. The bed was his own, the room was his own. Best and happiest of all, the Time before him was his own, to make amends in!

"I will live in the Past, the Present, and the Future!" Scrooge repeated, as he scrambled out of bed. "The Spirits of all Three shall strive within me. Oh Jacob Marley! Heaven, and the

Christmas Time be praised for this! I say it on
my knees, old Jacob, on my knees! "

He was so fluttered and so glowing with his
good intentions, that his broken voice would
scarcely answer to his call. He had been sobbing
violently in his conflict with the Spirit, and his
face was wet with tears.

" They are not torn down," cried Scrooge,
folding one of his bed-curtains in his arms, " they
are not torn down, rings and all. They are
here: I am here: the shadows of the things
that would have been, may be dispelled. They
will be. I know they will! "

His hands were busy with his garments all
this time : turning them inside out, putting
them on upside down, tearing them, mislaying
them, making them parties to every kind of
extravagance.

" I don't know what to do! " cried Scrooge,
laughing and crying in the same breath; and
making a perfect Laocoön of himself with his
stockings. " I am as light as a feather, I am as
happy as an angel, I am as merry as a schoolboy.
I am as giddy as a drunken man. A Merry Christmas to everybody! A Happy New Year to all
the world. Hallo here! Whoop! Hallo! "

He had frisked into the sitting-room, and was
now standing there: perfectly winded.

"There's the saucepan that the gruel was in!" cried Scrooge, starting off again, and frisking round the fireplace. "There's the door by which the Ghost of Jacob Marley entered! There's the corner where the Ghost of Christmas Present sat! There's the window where I saw the wandering Spirits! It's all right, it's all true, it all happened. Ha, ha, ha!"

Really, for a man who had been out of practice for so many years, it was a splendid laugh, a most illustrious laugh. The father of a long, long line of brilliant laughs!

"I don't know what day of the month it is!" said Scrooge. "I don't know how long I've been among the Spirits. I don't know anything. I'm quite a baby. Never mind. I don't care. I'd rather be a baby. Hallo! Whoop! Hallo here!"

He was checked in his transports by the churches ringing out the lustiest peals he had ever heard. Clash, clang, hammer, ding, dong, bell. Bell, dong, ding, hammer, clang, clash! Oh, glorious, glorious!

Running to the window, he opened it, and put out his head. No fog, no mist; clear, bright, jovial, stirring, cold; cold, piping for the blood to dance to; golden sunlight; heavenly sky; sweet fresh air; merry bells. Oh, glorious, glorious!

"What's to-day?" cried Scrooge, calling down-

ward to a boy in Sunday clothes, who perhaps
had loitered in to look about him.

"Eh?" returned the boy, with all his might
of wonder.

"What's to-day, my fine fellow?" said Scrooge.

"To-day!" replied the boy. "Why, CHRIST-
MAS DAY."

"It's Christmas Day!" said Scrooge to himself. "I haven't missed it. The Spirits have done
it all in one night. They can do anything they
like. Of course they can. Of course they can.
Hallo, my fine fellow!"

"Hallo!" returned the boy.

"Do you know the Poulterer's, in the next
street but one, at the corner?" Scrooge inquired.

"I should hope I did," replied the lad.

"An intelligent boy!" said Scrooge. "A remarkable boy! Do you know whether they've
sold the prize Turkey that was hanging up there?
Not the little prize Turkey: the big one?"

"What, the one as big as me?" returned the
boy.

"What a delightful boy!" said Scrooge. "It's
a pleasure to talk to him. Yes, my buck!"

"It's hanging there now," replied the boy.

"Is it?" said Scrooge. "Go and buy it."

"Walk-ER!" exclaimed the boy.

"No, no," said Scrooge, "I am in earnest.

Go and buy it, and tell 'em to bring it here, that
I may give them the direction where to take it.
Come back with the man, and I'll give you a
shilling. Come back with him in less than five
minutes, and I'll give you half-a-crown!"

The boy was off like a shot. He must have
had a steady hand at a trigger who could have
got a shot off half so fast.

"I'll send it to Bob Cratchit's!" whispered
Scrooge, rubbing his hands, and splitting with a
laugh. "He shan't know who sends it. It's
twice the size of Tiny Tim. Joe Miller never
made such a joke as sending it to Bob's will
be!"

The hand in which he wrote the address was
not a steady one, but write it he did, somehow,
and went down stairs to open the street door,
ready for the coming of the poulterer's man. As
he stood there, waiting his arrival, the knocker
caught his eye.

"I shall love it, as long as I live!" cried
Scrooge, patting it with his hand. "I scarcely
ever looked at it before. What an honest expression it has in its face! It's a wonderful knocker!
—Here's the Turkey. Hallo! Whoop! How are
you! Merry Christmas!"

It *was* a Turkey! He could never have stood
upon his legs, that bird. He would have snapped

'em short off in a minute, like sticks of sealing-wax.

"Why, it's impossible to carry that to Camden Town," said Scrooge. "You must have a cab."

The chuckle with which he said this, and the chuckle with which he paid for the Turkey, and the chuckle with which he paid for the cab, and the chuckle with which he recompensed the boy, were only to be exceeded by the chuckle with which he sat down breathless in his chair again, and chuckled till he cried.

Shaving was not an easy task, for his hand continued to shake very much; and shaving requires attention, even when you don't dance while you are at it. But if he had cut the end of his nose off, he would have put a piece of sticking-plaster over it, and been quite satisfied.

He dressed himself "all in his best," and at last got out into the streets. The people were by this time pouring forth, as he had seen them with the Ghost of Christmas Present; and walking with his hands behind him, Scrooge regarded every one with a delighted smile. He looked so irresistibly pleasant, in a word, that three or four good-humoured fellows said, "Good morning, sir! A Merry Christmas to you!" And Scrooge said often afterwards, that of all the blithe sounds he had ever heard, those were the blithest in his ears.

He had not gone far, when coming on towards him he beheld the portly gentleman who had walked into his counting-house the day before and said "Scrooge and Marley's, I believe?" It sent a pang across his heart to think how this old gentleman would look upon him when they met; but he knew what path lay straight before him, and he took it.

"My dear sir," said Scrooge, quickening his pace, and taking the old gentleman by both his hands. "How do you do? I hope you succeeded yesterday. It was very kind of you. A Merry Christmas to you, sir!"

"Mr. Scrooge?"

"Yes," said Scrooge. "That is my name, and I fear it may not be pleasant to you. Allow me to ask your pardon. And will you have the goodness—" here Scrooge whispered in his ear.

"Lord bless me!" cried the gentleman, as if his breath were gone. "My dear Mr. Scrooge, are you serious?"

"If you please," said Scrooge. "Not a farthing less. A great many back-payments are included in it, I assure you. Will you do me that favour?"

"My dear sir," said the other, shaking hands with him. "I don't know what to say to such munifi—"

" Don't say anything, please," retorted Scrooge.
" Come and see me. Will you come and see
me ? "

" I will! " cried the old gentleman. And it
was clear he meant to do it.

" Thank'ee," said Scrooge. " I am much
obliged to you. I thank you fifty times. Bless
you! "

He went to church, and walked about the
streets, and watched the people hurrying to and
fro, and patted children on the head, and questioned beggars, and looked down into the kitchens
of houses, and up to the windows; and found
that everything could yield him pleasure. He
had never dreamed that any walk—that anything—could give him so much happiness. In
the afternoon, he turned his steps towards his
nephew's house.

He passed the door a dozen times, before he
had the courage to go up and knock. But he
made a dash, and did it.

" Is your master at home, my dear? " said
Scrooge to the girl. Nice girl! Very.

" Yes, sir."

" Where is he, my love? " said Scrooge.

" He's in the dining-room, sir, along with
mistress. I'll show you upstairs, if you please."

" Thank'ee. He knows me," said Scrooge,

with his hand already on the dining-room lock. " I'll go in here, my dear."

He turned it gently, and sidled his face in, round the door. They were looking at the table (which was spread out in great array); for these young housekeepers are always nervous on such points, and like to see that everything is right.

" Fred! " said Scrooge.

Dear heart alive, how his niece by marriage started! Scrooge had forgotten, for the moment, about her sitting in the corner with the footstool, or he wouldn't have done it, on any account.

" Why bless my soul! " cried Fred, " who's that? "

" It's I. Your uncle Scrooge. I have come to dinner. Will you let me in, Fred? "

Let him in! It is a mercy he didn't shake his arm off. He was at home in five minutes. Nothing could be heartier. His niece looked just the same. So did Topper when *he* came. So did the plump sister, when *she* came. So did every one when *they* came. Wonderful party, wonderful games, wonderful unanimity, won-der-ful happiness!

But he was early at the office next morning. Oh he was early there. If he could only be there first, and catch Bob Cratchit coming late! That was the thing he had set his heart upon.

And he did it; yes, he did! The clock struck

nine. No Bob. A quarter past. No Bob. He was full eighteen minutes and a half behind his time. Scrooge sat with his door wide open, that he might see him come into the Tank.

His hat was off, before he opened the door; his comforter too. He was on his stool in a jiffy; driving away with his pen, as if he were trying to overtake nine o'clock.

"Hallo!" growled Scrooge, in his accustomed voice as near as he could feign it. "What do you mean by coming here at this time of day?"

"I am very sorry, sir," said Bob. "I *am* behind my time."

"You are?" repeated Scrooge. "Yes. I think you are. Step this way, sir, if you please."

"It's only once a year, sir," pleaded Bob, appearing from the Tank. "It shall not be repeated. I was making rather merry yesterday, sir."

"Now, I'll tell you what, my friend," said Scrooge, "I am not going to stand this sort of thing any longer. And therefore," he continued, leaping from his stool, and giving Bob such a dig in the waistcoat that he staggered back into the Tank again: "and therefore I am about to raise your salary!"

Bob trembled, and got a little nearer to the ruler. He had a momentary idea of knocking Scrooge down with it; holding him; and calling

"I am about to raise your salary!"

to the people in the court for help and a strait-
waistcoat.

"A Merry Christmas, Bob!" said Scrooge,
with an earnestness that could not be mistaken,
as he clapped him on the back. "A merrier
Christmas, Bob, my good fellow, than I have
given you for many a year! I'll raise your salary,
and endeavour to assist your struggling family,
and we will discuss your affairs this very afternoon, over a Christmas bowl of smoking bishop,
Bob! Make up the fires, and buy another coal-
scuttle before you dot another i, Bob Cratchit!"

Scrooge was better than his word. He did it
all, and infinitely more; and to Tiny Tim, who

did NOT die, he was a second father. He became as good a friend, as good a master, and as good a man, as the good old City knew, or any other good old city, town, or borough, in the good old world. Some people laughed to see the alteration in him, but he let them laugh, and little heeded them; for he was wise enough to know that nothing ever happened on this globe for good, at which some people did not have their fill of laughter in the outset; and knowing that such as these would be blind anyway, he thought it quite as well that they should wrinkle up their eyes in grins, as have the malady in less attractive forms. His own heart laughed: and that was quite enough for him.

He had no further intercourse with Spirits, but lived upon the Total Abstinence Principle, ever afterwards; and it was always said of him, that he knew how to keep Christmas well, if any man alive possessed the knowledge. May that be truly said of us, and all of us! And so, as Tiny Tim observed, God Bless Us, Every One!

LIFE OF CHARLES DICKENS

WHENEVER we speak of an umbrella as a " gamp "; or say that a mean, grasping man is " a regular Scrooge "; that a podgy urchin is a " Fat Boy "; that someone who trusts to luck and to " something turning up " is " another Micawber "; that a boy who has no bashfulness about passing in his plate is " an Oliver Twist "; that a person full of tricks is " an Artful Dodger "; that a cheerful sanguine man is " another Mark Tapley "; or express consent or agreement by the use of the phrase " Barkis is willin' "; or rally a grumbler with the name " Mrs. Gummidge "; we testify to the fame of the novelist, Charles Dickens. For only a writer of outstanding merit and special qualities of human appeal could make the names of his characters and the things they said

Familiar in our mouths as household words.

Biographies of literary men are usually the driest of dust, and the facts of their outward lives seem, at first, to have little or nothing to do with that wonderful inward world which their writings reveal to all who love them. But, in the case of a writer of fiction, it is right that we should make some enquiry into the circumstances of his outward life, because, if he is really a great writer, he bases all his narratives upon actual experiences; and he models each of his characters upon someone who was personally known to him, although he does not draw exact portraits so that anyone shall be able to say, "This is a picture of so-and-so."

When Dickens lavished all his wealth of affection upon the character of Little Nell in *The Old Curiosity Shop*, he was thinking of the younger sister of his wife, Mary Hogarth, for whom he had a passionate love and who died in her youth; but there was no parallel between the outward lives of the two girls. In his story *David Copperfield* we read how the little boy found work with a wine-merchant, his duty being to paste the labels upon the bottles. In real life the boy, Charles Dickens, was employed at a blacking warehouse where it was his duty " to cover the pots of paste-blacking; first with a piece of oil-paper, and then with a piece of blue paper; to tie them round with a string; and then to clip the paper close and neat all round, until it looked as smart as a pot of ointment from an apothecary's

shop." The cases are parallel, not identical, so far
as external circumstances are concerned; but both
of these delicate, sensitive little boys, the real and
the imaginary, would have the same feelings of degradation, and they provoke the same pity in the
mind of the reader. So Dickens gives reality and
truthfulness to his writings, touching the real
with the glow of his imagination, but rarely
departing from what is possible and probable,
telling always of something which, if it had not
happened, *might* have happened.

Charles Dickens was born at Portsea, a suburb
of Portsmouth, on the 7th of February, 1812.
He died on the 9th of June, 1870, so that his life
was comparatively short; but in actual achieve-
ment and intensity of living his life was much
longer than its fifty-eight years. His birthplace
and his family were equally obscure, but he lived
to win fame throughout the whole of the English-
speaking world and beyond it, and was finally
laid to rest in Westminster Abbey, the burial-
place of some of the most famous men of his race.

His father was a clerk in the Navy Pay-office,
on a salary of £80 a year, and was stationed for
two years at Portsmouth. Then, in the winter of
1814, the family moved to London, when the
ground was covered with snow, as the novelist
always remembered, and two years later to

Chatham, where they lived for five years. His
mother was his first teacher, but at the age of
seven he went to a private school kept by a
Baptist minister. He was a quick, clever child,
and his father used to make him sit on a tall
chair in the office and recite ballads or tell stories
to the other clerks. At home he devoured all the
books on which he could lay his hands, including
Robinson Crusoe, *The Vicar of Wakefield*, *Don
Quixote*, *Tom Jones*, *Roderick Random*, and other
fiction of a bygone time. He tells us in *David
Copperfield* how he played at the characters in
these books; for he was a born actor as well as
a teller of tales.

When the elder Dickens was eventually sum-
moned to London to work at Somerset House, the
family settled in Camden Town. It has been said
that in the shiftless, sentimental Mr. Micawber
of *David Copperfield* we have a " portrait " of
Dickens' father. This is only partially true, of
course, as in other cases; but the fact remains
that John Dickens was most unfitted to be the
father of a family of six, and his bad habits had
reduced his family to a state of extreme poverty.
At last he was arrested for debt and carried off
to the Marshalsea prison, where Charles visited
him. The boy now became closely acquainted
with the pawn-shop, while his books were sold to

buy food. He was sent to the blacking warehouse already mentioned, where he earned some six shillings weekly and was forced to associate with boys of low character, and dined usually on " a saveloy and a penny loaf; sometimes a four-penny plate of beef from a cook's shop; some-times a plate of bread and cheese, and a glass of beer, from a miserable old public-house over the way."

" Once I remember," Dickens afterwards wrote, " tucking my own bread (which I had brought from home in the morning) under my arm, wrapped up in a piece of paper like a book, and going into the best dining-room in Johnson's à-la-mode beef-house in Clare Court, Drury Lane, and magnificently ordering a small plate of à-la-mode beef to eat with it. What the waiter thought of such a strange little apparition coming in all alone, I don't know; but I can see him now staring at me as I ate my dinner and bringing up the other waiter to look. I gave him a halfpenny, and I wish now that he hadn't taken it."

His mother and the rest of the Dickens family joined the father in the prison, and a back attic was found for Charles in a neighbouring street.

---

[1] Quoted in John Forster's *Life*. The passage ought to be compared with part of Chapter XI. of *David Copperfield*.

The family were waited upon by a little servant girl, brought from Chatham workhouse, who also had a lodging near the prison. Charles breakfasted and had supper in the prison, whose gates were closed at ten o'clock. During this impressionable time he spent many hours in wandering the streets of London and gathering at first hand that intimate knowledge of the life, especially the lower life, of the great city, which he used so freely in his books, and which made him the most complete and famous of those writers who have described the life of London. Nearly all the people with whom he was closely acquainted at this time appear in his books.

A legacy from a relative enabled the Dickens family to leave the Marshalsea, and, to his great delight, Charles was sent to a private school. Then he entered the office of a Gray's Inn solicitor, and spent the greater part of his spare time in the Reading Room of the British Museum. He learnt shorthand, and became a reporter in London police courts, and later in the Press Gallery of the House of Commons. In May 1865, speaking at a Press dinner, he said:

"I went into the Gallery of the House of Commons as a Parliamentary reporter when I was a boy, and I left it nigh thirty years ago. I have pursued the calling of a reporter under circumstances of which many of my brethren here can form no adequate conception. I have often transcribed for the printer, from my shorthand notes, important public speeches in which the strictest accuracy was required, and a mistake in which would have been to a young man severely compromising, writing on the palm of my hand, by the light of a dark lantern, in a post-chaise and four, galloping through a wild country, and through the dead of night, at the then surprising rate of fifteen miles an hour. . . . I have worn my knees by writing on them on the old back row of the old gallery of the House of Commons; and I have worn my feet by standing to write in a preposterous pen in the old House of Lords, where we used to be huddled together like so many sheep—kept in waiting, say, until the woolsack might want re-stuffing. . . . I do verily believe I have been upset in almost every description of vehicle known in this country. I have been, in my time, belated on miry byroads, towards the small hours, forty or fifty miles from London, in a wheelless carriage, with exhausted horses and drunken post-boys, and have got back in time for publication."

In 1835 he began to write short light sketches or articles for the *Evening Chronicle*, and in the following year these papers were published in book form under the title of *Sketches by Boz*. At this time he began to issue in shilling paper-backed numbers *The Posthumous Papers of the Pickwick Club*, and at about the same time he married Miss Catherine Hogarth, and took into his new home his wife's sister Mary to whom reference has already been made. Wonderful success attended *The Pickwick Papers*, especially after the appearance of Sam Weller in Part V., and before they were completed he began the writing of *Oliver Twist*. By this time he was without contradiction the foremost literary man of his time, and was praised and fêted by all kinds of people. The rest of his life consisted of a course of almost unbroken literary success. He made a great deal of money, and often spent rather more than he made, for he was generous and hospitable to a fault, and he was, moreover, keenly desirous of doing the very best he could for his growing family.

Before *Oliver Twist* was concluded *Nicholas Nickleby* was begun, presenting the immortal schoolmaster Squeers of Dotheboys Hall, and the talkative Mrs. Nickleby, who is said to be a " portrait " of the author's mother. Then came *The Old Curiosity Shop*, in which appear the Marchioness, recalling the sharp little drudge from Chatham Workhouse, the wandering Punch and Judy, Dick Swiveller and the pathetic Little Nell. In *Barnaby Rudge*, a historical novel of the time of the Gordon Riots, he modelled his work upon Scott, who had died some few years before, but the reader remembers the poor innocent Barnaby and his raven,[1] as well as the pretty maiden, Dolly Varden, and Simon Tappertit, better than the history of that troubled time.

In 1842, Dickens paid his first visit to America, and was received everywhere with the greatest enthusiasm, but afterwards offended his hosts by some frank criticism of their mode of life which appeared in his new novel *Martin Chuzzlewit*, the story which contained Mr. Pecksniff, Mrs. Gamp, Betsey Prig, and "Mrs Harris." Near the end of 1843 he wrote the *Christmas Carol*, which did not bring in as much money as he expected; so he went off to Italy where living was cheaper, and while occupying a villa on the outskirts of Genoa he wrote *The Chimes*, the second of the series of "Christmas Stories." For a short period during the year 1846 he was editor of the *Daily News*, but soon gave up the task and went abroad again, this time to Lausanne on the Lake of Geneva, where he began to write *Dombey and*

[1] There was a real Grip the Raven, the playmate of the novelist's own children.

Son. This story was so successful that he was able to return to England, settling at Broadstairs, and commencing the composition of *David Copperfield*.

"Of all my books," writes the author, "I like this the best; like many fond parents, I have my favourite child, and his name is David Copperfield." Here we meet with Mr. and Mrs. Micawber and their family, Peggotty, Barkis, who was "willin'," Betsy Trotwood, Thomas Traddles, Mrs. Gummidge, "Little Em'ly," and Uriah Heep, whose names and sayings have passed into the national language and life. "Micawber," writes G. K. Chesterton, "is the superman. We can only walk round and round him wondering what we shall say. All the critics of Dickens, when all is said and done, have only walked round and round Micawber wondering what they should say. I am myself, at this moment, walking round and round Micawber wondering what I shall say. And I have not found out yet."

The story of *Bleak House* (1852) centres round a Chancery suit and is somewhat dreary and rambling, and *Hard Times* (1854) is spoilt for many readers as a tale by being a kind of social tract, which no novel has any right to be. But in the following year, about the time when he

settled at Gad's Hill, near Rochester, Dickens
began the story of *Little Dorrit*, a tale of the
Marshalsea, which was followed in 1859 by *A
Tale of Two Cities*, a story of the French Revolu-
tion, carefully constructed—" the best story I
have ever written "—in which incident matters
more than characterisation, and from which the
peculiar Dickensian humour is absent. The story
is full of vivid word-pictures, one of the most
notable being that of the storming of the Bastille,
and is worked up to a wonderful scenic climax,
theatrical indeed, but full of power. Then came
Great Expectations (1861), followed by *Our Mutual
Friend* (1864), both of which show us the lower
reaches of the Thames, and the life of the boat-
men and loafers of the world's greatest port. The
early part of the former book is as full of personal
interest as the first portion of *David Copperfield*,
while Pumblechook, Joe Gargery, Mr. Wemmick
and Mr. Jaggers take a worthy place in the
Dickens gallery of immortals.

In November, 1867, Dickens, being in great
need of money, made a tour in America, giving
in various cities readings from his own works
which were overwhelmingly popular. The strain
of the work was very heavy, and he broke down ;
but chiefly for financial reasons he resumed the
readings when he returned to England, greatly

against the wishes of his friends, and continued at this exhausting task up to March 1870. The next three months were spent on *The Mystery of Edwin Drood*, which he did not live to finish.

On the 8th of June he spent a long morning writing in the châlet in his garden, and at the dinner-table suddenly changed colour, and showed marked signs of distress. His sister-in-law, Miss Georgina Hogarth, asked him if he were ill, and he replied, " Yes, very ill," but added that he would finish the meal and afterwards go on to London. " Come and lie down," she said. " Yes, on the ground," he replied very distinctly; these were the last words he spoke, and he slid from her arms and fell upon the floor. He was put to bed, and died on the evening of the following day. He had left instructions in his will to the effect that he was to be buried quietly and without display, and though he desired to lie in the small graveyard under the shadow of Rochester Castle wall, his relatives, after pressure, accepted the offer of a grave in Poets' Corner, Westminster Abbey.

" Dickens had no artistic ideals worth speaking about," writes a critic. " The sympathy of his readers was the one thing he cared about, and he went straight for it, through the avenue of the emotions. In personality, intensity, and

F

range of creative genius he can hardly be said
to have any modern rival. His creations live,
move, and have their being about us constantly
like those of Homer, Virgil, Chaucer, Rabelais,
Cervantes, Shakespeare, Bunyan, Molière, and
Sir Walter Scott."

THOUGHTS AND QUESTIONS

(To be used in a second or subsequent reading of
A Christmas Carol)

AUTHOR'S NOTE

1. What do you think was the " Ghost of an Idea " mentioned in the Author's preliminary note?

2. What is meant by " laying " a ghost?

STAVE ONE

3. What is meant by " Scrooge's name was good upon 'Change "?

4. Why do *you* think we speak of " as dead as a door-nail "?

5. Look up in a good dictionary the meaning of: Executor, administrator, assign, and legatee.

6. Did Dickens think that Hamlet was mad?

7. Why didn't Scrooge paint out Marley's name?

8. Think of a kind, gentle, genial, jolly man and

describe him on the model of the paragraph which begins, " Oh! But he was a tight-fisted hand at the grindstone, Scrooge!" Do not worry if you have to miss out a little of the description.

9. Can you find any " poetry " in the paragraph which begins, " External heat and cold "? If so, write it out in " poetry " form.

10. How could Scrooge have " come down handsomely "? Did he finally do so?

11. Read aloud, very slowly, the sentence, " It was cold, bleak, biting weather . . . to warm them." What is the effect of the words?

12. Which speech of Scrooge's nephew sums up the Dickens view of Christmas? Can you assent to each sentence of this creed or declaration?

13. What is your opinion of the nephew's persistence?

14. Note that Bedlam is a shorter form of Bethlehem, a hospital for lunatics in London.

15. What did the gentleman do who " presented his credentials "?

16. Why did he lay down the pen again when he re-echoed Scrooge's words " plenty of prisons "?

17. Why had Scrooge " an improved opinion of himself " after the interview with the two gentlemen?

18. What do you think a " flaring link " was? Why " *misanthropic* ice "?

19. Find an excellent double picture in the paragraph which begins, " Meanwhile the fog and darkness."

20. If you do not know the story of St. Dunstan and the Devil, can you make it up from the hints here given?

21. What reminiscence of Dickens' own life is there in the paragraph beginning, " The clerk promised that he would "? Note that Bob Cratchit had to walk three or four miles to his home.

22. What is a " *melancholy* dinner "?

23. What is the light " round a bad lobster in a dark cellar "?

24. What good feature in Scrooge's character can be discovered from the account of his entry into his house and the incident of the knocker?

25. For the " ancient Prophet's rod " look up Exodus vii. 10-12.

26. What is the most dramatic touch in the description of the entry of Marley's Ghost? And what is the most creepy thing about the description of Marley himself?

27. How do you think Scrooge conducts himself at the meeting?

28. What do you think is the meaning of the sentence, " It is required of every man that the spirit within him should walk abroad among his fellow-men, and travel far and wide "?

29. Consider the sentence, " Oh! captive, bound," etc. What is the meaning of the phrase " *for* this earth "? Is the Phantom calling himself or Scrooge a " captive bound "?

30. Do you think that the way in which Dickens tells of the interview with the ghost is really creepy? How does he avoid real " creepiness "?

STAVE TWO

31. Why is this story divided into " staves " instead of the ordinary chapters?

32. What are " *ferret* eyes "?

33. What is a " repeater "?

34. What do you think was the author's opinion of " a mere United States security "?

35. Compare the description of the boy reading by the fire with the picture on page 41. What characters do you think the artist shows? In what book would he read of Ali Baba? and of the Sultan's Groom and the Genii?

Note that Valentine and Orson were the heroes of a fifteenth-century romance.

36. What is meant by, " from his shoes to his organ of benevolence "?

37. Look up " negus " in the dictionary.

38. When Scrooge says, " I should like to be able to say a word or two to my clerk just now," he makes the second sign of repentance. Can you find the first?

39. What is a dowerless girl?

40. The " celebrated herd in the poem" was that of Wordsworth's lines:

> The cattle are grazing,
> Their heads never raising;
> There are forty, feeding like one!

These lines occur in the poem *Lines written in March.*

41. Where did Scrooge really see these spirits?

STAVE THREE

42. In the description of the Ghost of Christmas Present, what is the meaning of the antique scabbard with no sword in it?

43. What were the " more than eighteen hundred " of the brothers of the Phantom?

44. Why is a *soft* snowball a " better-natured missile far than many a wordy jest "?

45. What do you think the prettiest picture in the description of the contents of the fruiterers' shops?

46. What do you like best in the description of the grocer's shop? What do you see in grocers' shops to-day that Dickens would not see?

47. Why did people send their Christmas dinners to the bakers' shops? Who had been objecting to this?

48. Perhaps the finest picture of a Christmas day's festivity is that beginning, " Then up rose Mrs. Cratchit."

49. Where are black swans to be found? Note that when they open their wings you can see their beautiful *white* feathers—but not till then.

50. What would be wrong if the pudding broke in turning out?

51. Why " a laundress's next door to that "?

52. What is the most natural sentence in the paragraph which begins, " Oh, a wonderful pudding! "?

53. What did the Spirit mean by " the Insect on the leaf "?

54. Note what can be done with some of Dickens' descriptive sentences:

Upon a dismal reef of sunken rock,
Some league or so from (the resounding) shore,
On which the waters dashed the wild year through,
A solitary lighthouse stood. Great heaps
Of sea weed clung around its base, and birds—
Born of the wind, as sea-weed of the waves—
Rose and fell round it, like the waves they skimmed.

Try to do this with other descriptive passages.

55. In what particular opinion did Mrs. Cratchit and Scrooge's nephew's wife agree?

56. Here is another descriptive bit:

She was pretty, exceedingly pretty,
With a dimpled, surprised-looking, capital face:
And a ripe little mouth, that seemed made to be kissed—
As no doubt it was!
She had all kinds of good little dots round her chin,
That whenever she laughed peeped out and then in,
And a pair of the sunniest eyes you e'er saw.

And so on.

57. Why did Scrooge's nephew say of his uncle, " He don't lose much of a dinner "?

58. What does the author mean by, " It was a done thing between him and Scrooge's nephew "?

59. Note how these lines fall into rhythm:

The Spirit stood beside sick-beds, and they were cheerful;
On foreign lands, and they were close at home;
By struggling men (grown) patient in their hope;
By poverty, and it was (passing) rich.

*F

60. Was the Ghost of Christmas Present concerned only with Christmas Day? How do you know?

61. What feeling does the author show in the paragraph beginning, "They were a boy and girl"?

STAVE FOUR

62. Is Dickens drawing upon his imagination in the description of a London slum which begins, "They left the busy scene"?

63. Do you think that Scrooge really needed the lesson of Stave Four? If not, why do you think so?

64. What does the last sentence of Stave Four tell you about Scrooge's visions?

65. Scrooge did not see the Ghost of Christmas Yet To Come. Can you invent one, and after considering the description of Christmas Present, suggest any improvement or alterations in his ways and thoughts? Or does Christmas Present please you in every way?

STAVE FIVE

66. Laocoön appears in the old Greek story of the Tale of Troy. He had been a priest of Apollo, but having angered the god, he and his two sons were attacked by writhing serpents while preparing to sacrifice a bull at the altar of Neptune, to whose service Laocoön had transferred himself. The strangling of the priest and his sons is shown in the famous marble group in the Vatican at Rome.

67. Why was the poulterer's shop open on Christmas morning?

68. If Scrooge had lived to-day, whose name would he have used in place of Joe Miller?

69. Which person or persons in this story do you like best, and why? Who was the kindest, the jolliest, the funniest, the most dreadful? Think out a future for your favourite character or characters, with good fortune and happiness in it. In what way or ways do you think Scrooge altered his mode of life? Whom would you have to succeed Scrooge in his business? What happened to Topper? How do you think the new Scrooge would make his will? Don't you think it a pity he should continue to be called Scrooge?

THE "CHRISTMAS CAROL"

A FAMOUS Scotsman wrote to Charles Dickens after the publication of the *Christmas Carol*: "Blessings on your kind heart! You should be happy yourself, for you may be sure you have done more good by this little publication, fostered more kindly feelings, and prompted more positive acts of benevolence, than can be traced to all the pulpits of Christendom since Christmas 1842."

"Who can listen," wrote the English author, W. M. Thackeray, "to objectors regarding such a book as this? It seems to me a national benefit, and to every man and woman who reads it a personal kindness."

"There was, indeed," wrote Dickens' own friend and biographer, John Forster, "nobody that had not some interest in the message of the *Christmas Carol*. It told the selfish man to rid himself of selfishness; the just man to make himself generous; and the good-natured man to enlarge the sphere of his good nature. Its cheery voice of faith and hope, ringing from one end of the island to the other, carried pleasant warning alike to all, that if the duties of Christmas were wanting, no good could come of its outward observances; that it must shine upon the cold hearth and warm it, and into the sorrowful heart and comfort it; *that it must be kindness, benevolence, charity, mercy, and forbearance, or its plum-pudding would turn to bile, and its roast beef be indigestible.*

" Nor could any man have said it with the same appropriateness as Dickens. What was marked in him to the last was manifest now. He had identified himself with Christmas fancies. Its life and spirits, its humour in riotous abundance, of right belonged to him. Its imaginations, as well as its kindly thoughts, were his; and its privilege to light up with some sort of comfort the squalidest places he had made his own. Christmas Day was not more social or welcome; New Year's Day not more new; Twelfth Night not more full of characters. The duty of diffusing enjoyment had never been taught by a more abundant, mirthful, thoughtful, ever-seasonable writer."

The words printed above in italic ought to be carefully noted, because they sum up so well the central idea of Charles Dickens' story. He did not invent Christmas feasting and jollity. He found these already in full swing, and he heartily approved of all the mirth, good-cheer and sociability. But he bade the revellers consider whether they were merely indulging in eating and drinking for greedy and selfish reasons, without a thought for the true meaning of Christmas, and the good-will of which the angels sang to the shepherds at Bethlehem. Moreover, if we read the story aright, we find that he does not look upon Christmas-time as a pleasant oasis in a desert formed by the rest of the year. He would have it not merely a time of good-will, but a yearly reminder that good-will ought to last throughout the year, a time when men of constant good-will should be more than usually kindly and when men of ill-will should make a fresh start for the coming year in the exercise of benevolence and kindliness, *and should thereafter keep it up.* Scrooge does not fall back after Twelfth Day. Christmas, or the visit of the ghosts, has taught him a lasting lesson, and future Christmases would be to him welcome opportunities for taking stock of his new mode of life and altered outlook, a milestone on a journey to the end of a life which his fellow-men would call truly blessed.

It is a hopeful sign that Scrooge was already old, and a sub-title for the story might very well be *It is never too Late to Mend.* But we are made to feel very keenly the tragedy of his lost years and opportunities, and we cannot dismiss the story as a tale meant only for hardened old skinflints. It is a tale for the young, containing a very serious warning of the misery that will most certainly attend upon a youth and early manhood or womanhood spent entirely in satisfaction of self, and the pursuit of gain or foolish pleasure. Scrooge's early life had inflicted pain and misery upon many people, and all his new resolutions could not undo what had been done. The story has a happy ending, but it is a tragedy rather than a comedy—a hopeful, wise tragedy, nevertheless.

We cannot read *A Christmas Carol* without feeling that we have made the personal acquaintance of the author. It is good to know a man of this stamp—to feel, as it were, the grasp of his hand, to join in his hearty harmless laugh, to share in the pity, mercy, and kindliness which fill his heart and overflow into his deeds, to share also in his indignation against wrong and cruelty and meanness, and especially against those who cause to suffer any of "these little ones" whom the "mighty Founder of Christmas" made the object of his especial love and care.

DICKENS AND DRAMA

WITH SPECIAL REFERENCE TO

"A CHRISTMAS CAROL"

CHARLES DICKENS was not only a writer. He was also an actor of considerable ability. This is not surprising, for he projects himself into his characters. For the moment he is not merely *writing* of Scrooge; he *is* Scrooge. It is this dramatic quality of his writing which makes it so real and appealing.

Not long after the publication of *A Christmas Carol*, a play was founded upon it and acted in London at the Adelphi Theatre. Dickens went to see it. He praised the man who acted Bob Cratchit, but he did not enjoy the play very much. If we think the matter out a little we can understand his dissatisfaction. Bob Cratchit had a very real existence in the mind of his creator, and the man who personated the poor and lovable clerk, however careful and conscientious an actor he might be, remained himself rather than Bob Cratchit. No doubt he occasionally did or said something which Dickens would know the real Bob Cratchit would never do; and we can imagine that the longer the author looked at the play the more impatient he would become. Perhaps it would have been better if he had closed his eyes and merely listened; but even then he would probably have detected some tone or inflection of voice which would annoy him. It was all very harassing, for the creator of a character is a very sensitive person indeed, and perhaps, after all, it would have been better if Dickens had stayed away from the Adelphi Theatre when *A Christmas Carol* was on the boards.

It was quite a different matter when Charles Dickens himself gave a reading from the book. In these circumstances the audience was asked to imagine the appearance of Bob Cratchit and Tiny Tim and the rest of them (and each person would have his *own* mental picture—a poor thing, perhaps, but his own), while the creator of these immortal characters showed, by means of his wonderful voice, what they said, and how they said it. Nothing came between the picture and the observer. There was no actor to make the wrong gesture or grimace, to sit down or stand up at the wrong moment, or to bring into the representation anything that would divert the mind of the listener. Now Dickens often gave public readings from his book, to the intense enjoyment of tens of thousands of English and American people—and one of the favourite readings was either the whole of the *Carol* or selected scenes from it, such as Bob Cratchit's Christmas Dinner. This was the best way, apart from reading, to help people to see (in imagination) and hear (in reality) the people whose sayings and doings had become in such a short time so wonderfully familiar to nearly all Britons and Americans. It must have been a memorable experience to hear Dickens conjure up in a few well-chosen words the scene in Bob Cratchit's kitchen, the phrases falling slowly from his lips so as to allow the imagination of the hearers time to work:

> They were not a handsome family; they were not well dressed; their shoes were far from being water-proof; their clothes were scanty; and Peter might have known, and very likely did, the inside of a pawnbroker's. But, they were happy, grateful, pleased with one another, and contented with the time; and when they faded, and looked happier yet in the bright sprinklings of the Spirit's torch at parting, Scrooge had his eye upon them, and especially on Tiny Tim, until the last.

These Dickens readings were immensely popular on both sides of the Atlantic—crowded audiences, hushed and rapt attention, deep emotion, enthusiastic applause, followed by intense exhaustion, and sometimes complete collapse, on the part of the author-reader. Besides the *Carol* he read scenes from *Pickwick*, the trial-scene being first favourite, *The Chimes*, Paul Dombey's death from *Dombey and Son*, "Boots at Holly-Tree Inn," [1] "Richard Doubledick" [1] from *The Seven Poor Travellers*, and the scenes from *Martin Chuzzlewit* in which Mrs. Gamp appears.

Dickens often wrote home immediately after one of his readings in a distant town, for he always felt keenly the separation from his family, and always hurried back to them as quickly as he could. He writes from Dublin on one of these occasions:

You can hardly imagine (the scene). All the way from the hotel to the Rotunda (a mile) I had to contend against the stream of people who were turned away. When I got there they had broken the glass of the pay-boxes and were offering £5 freely for a stall. Half of my platform had to be taken down and people heaped in among the ruins. You never saw such a scene. . . . They had offered frantic prices for stalls. Eleven bank-notes were thrust into a pay-box at one time for eleven stalls. Our men were flattened against walls and squeezed against beams. Ladies stood all night with their chins against my platform. Other ladies sat all night upon my steps. We turned away people enough to make immense houses for a week.

From Boston, U.S.A., he writes:

To-morrow fortnight we propose being at the Falls of Niagara. I have got to know the *Carol* so well that

[1] See the volume in the "Kings' Treasuries" series entitled *The Wreck of the Golden Mary, and Other Stories*.

I can't remember it, and occasionally go dodging about in the wildest manner to pick up lost pieces. They took it so tremendously last night that I was stopped every five minutes. One poor young girl in mourning burst into a passion of grief about Tiny Tim, and was taken out. We had a fine house and, in the interval, while I was out, they covered the little table with flowers.

It is a good exercise to take one of the scenes from *A Christmas Carol* and write it out in the form of a play, even if you do not really act it. It helps you to realise the details of the scene and the doings of the people better than merely reading the account as Dickens wrote it. Let us take, for example, the Christmas Dinner, which might be set out in the following manner:

MRS. CRATCHIT'S CHRISTMAS DINNER

SCENE: *The kitchen of Bob Cratchit's four-roomed house*

Mrs. Cratchit, in a twice-turned gown, but brave in ribbons, lays the cloth, assisted by her second daughter, Belinda, also brave in ribbons. Master Peter Cratchit, in a monstrous shirt-collar, plunges a fork into a saucepan of potatoes. Two smaller Cratchits, boy and girl, burst in.

Both together. Mother, we've been to the baker's and—

Mrs. C. Well, dearies, what about it?

Both together. We smelt a goose cooking and knew
   by the smell that it must be ours.   How fine
   our Peter is!

   [*Peter looks so pleased that to hide his pleasure
      he blows the fire.   The potatoes bubble up
      and knock loudly at the saucepan-lid to
      be let out and peeled.*[1]

Mrs. C. What has ever got your precious father,
   then?   And your brother, Tiny Tim!   And
   Martha warn't as late last Christmas Day by
   half-an-hour.

A Voice. Here's Martha, mother!

   Martha enters.

Two Young Cratchits.   Here's Martha, mother!
   Hurrah!   There's *such* a goose, Martha!

Mrs. C. [*kissing Martha a dozen times and busily
   taking off her shawl*].   Why, bless your heart
   alive, my dear, how late you are!

Martha. We'd a deal of work to finish up last
   night, and had to clear away this morning,
   mother.

Mrs. C. Well, never mind, so long as you *are*
   come.   Sit ye down before the fire, my dear,
   and have a warm, Lord bless ye!

   [1] Evidently boiled in their jackets.   There is a knotty
question here!

Two Young Cratchits. No, no! There's father coming. Hide, Martha, hide!

Perhaps you can now finish this play for yourselves, following the text of the story very closely, missing no details either of what we might call the stage directions, which are printed above in italic, or of the conversations.

There are other good dramatic scenes in the book, such as The Nephew's Party, and The Meeting of Scrooge and Marley, while two contrasting scenes can be constructed, the first showing Scrooge and Bob as in the beginning of the story, the second showing the same two characters in the office after Scrooge's conversion.

ADDITIONAL NOTE

[THE figures shown in the picture at the head of Stave Two ought to arouse curiosity in the books with which the boy has made himself familiar. It will be easy to get *Robinson Crusoe* and *Tales from the Arabian Nights* to find out about the doings of Ali Baba and the Sultan and the Genii or Jinns. But the story of the brothers Valentine and Orson, which explains the presence of the armed knight and the bear in the picture, is not so well known or so accessible. A prose rendering of the tale is therefore given below. In one old verse or ballad form of the story the brother of Valentine is referred to as Ursine. This form of his name is helpful, for it reminds us of the Latin name *ursa* for a bear. But we shall retain the more usual form, namely, Orson.]

THE TALE OF VALENTINE AND ORSON

I

ONE morning, in the merry spring-time—it was, indeed, the season when holy clerks sang their matins to Saint Valentine—the King of France set out a hunting in the forest of Artois. A courtly train of gallant peers attended him, and the hills and valleys echoed with their loud and cheerful cries and the sound of their hunting horns.

On they went through a deep and lonely forest, when suddenly, in a lonely dell they found a little child. It was lying upon a scarlet kerchief of fine silk and was wrapped round with a golden mantle pinned with a silver pin. The sight surprised them all, and the courtiers looked keenly round expecting to find the mother — but no mother could be found.

Then King Pepin himself drew near, and as he stood gazing the pretty babe looked up and smiled and stretched out its little hands. " The child is passing fair," said the monarch, " and must be of gentle blood—perhaps some prince's heir. Take him to the court with all care and let him be christened Valentine in honour of this day."

This was done. The little babe was placed in the tender care of the best nurse that could be found and grew up well loved by the king and all his lords. He became so strong and bold that before he had reached manhood he was made a knight and earnestly begged of the king, as a boon, that he should be given the first adventure that might befall. To this the king consented readily.

Not many days later three pilgrims in grey gowns came weeping before the king. " We come, sire," they said, " from the forest of Artois with weak and weary feet to tell you that a savage boy lives in those deep and dreamy woods, whose fierceness makes all around afraid. He lives with bears in their lair and drinks the blood of men. He has more than the strength of a wild beast joined with the cunning of a man, and only one in arms could hope to subdue him."

Then the king gave this adventure to Sir Valentine, who forthwith rode out on a milk-white steed, clad in armour white as snow, and came with all haste to the forest. There he found the savage youth feeding like a beast on raw flesh. His long and matted hair hung down upon his shoulders; his eyes seemed to flash fire; his nails were like the talons of an eagle; his limbs were thick, strong and hairy; and he carried a dreadful club of knotted oak.

As soon as he saw Sir Valentine he gave a dreadful shout and leapt upon him with uplifted club; but he was met by the spear of the knight, which bore him to his knees. A second stroke laid him low, but he sprang up and dealt a terrible blow which missed the knight but broke his spear

to shivers. Sir Valentine leapt from his horse and
drew his sword which the savage gripped by the
blade and so received a ghastly wound which
angered him still more. Throwing his mighty
arms round the knight he wrestled with him and
laid him upon the ground. Up sprang Sir Valentine and the two fought with their fists until the
skill of the knight prevailed over savage strength
and rage. Then the victor bound the vanquished
savage with an iron chain and led him to court
tied to his horse's tail. Loss of blood had tamed
the savage and after a while he became Sir
Valentine's faithful servant and followed him
about like a dog, while he was known to all as
Orson, because he had lived with the bears.

II

ONE day the king prepared a sumptuous feast to
which he invited many great lords and dainty
dames. As the company feasted a foolish young
knight taunted Sir Valentine with his lowly
birth. The taunt angered the knight and he took
a vow never to rest till he had found his parents.
So he said good-bye to the king and his lords and
with Orson by his side set out on his adventures.
    They passed over hill and valley, moss and
moor, until they came to a bridge of brass across

a moat which surrounded a castle of marble with battlements of gold. Beneath the bridge were hung a hundred bells, so that if either man or beast passed across the chiming of the bells gave warning of their approach.

As soon as Sir Valentine rode upon the bridge the bells began to ring, and at the sound the gates were flung wide open and a huge giant stalked out. " Yield you," he roared, " or the wolves shall eat your flesh and the ravens drink your blood."

" Vain boaster," cried the knight, " I am come to set your captives free." Then the two closed in hideous clashing combat and after a while both knight and horse lay prone upon the bridge. The giant was about to give the final stroke when two thundering blows descended on his skull from Orson's club of knotted oak. The giant sank down with rolling eyes and two more blows despatched him.

Then Orson tenderly revived the knight and the two set out to explore the castle. Wherever they came, they found the blood and bones of murdered knights, and at last they reached a dungeon where they found a lady whose gentle eyes were dimmed with tears and cheeks pale with sorrow. Sir Valentine spoke gently to her, asking how he could serve her, and she replied:

" You see before you a childless mother and a wife without a mate. For twenty years have I lived in this place, the suffering captive of a monster, wishing for death. I am sister of a king and was wedded to a mighty prince with whom I lived in happiness for a twelvemonth and a day.

" But a treacherous priest spoke evil of me to my dear lord and I was driven from his castle with a single knight as my guard. Towards my brother's distant court I went, heavy with sorrow, and after much travel we came to a deep forest where twin boys were born to me.

" The elder was fair and as smooth as the newly-fallen snow, but the younger was dark and hairy like a little bear. As I lay on the earth a prowling bear burst from the wood and carried off the younger babe. I ran after the beast, but it outstripped me and I fell to the earth in a swoon. After a while the knight who had gone to seek help found and revived me, but neither of my pretty babes could be found. As we searched for them the giant of this castle came upon us and made us his captives."

" Now surely," said the wondering Valentine, " you are the Lady Bellisance, wife to the Grecian emperor and sister to King Pepin of France. Know then that I have often heard your story, that the treacherous priest died confessing his misdeeds, and that your husband has sought you long, and now lives a hermit for your sake. Moreover, do you know this cloak?" As he spoke he unwrapped a golden garment which was strapped to his horse. At the sight of it the lady swooned away.

But it was joy that overwhelmed her, and when she was tenderly revived she heard the wonderful story of the two brothers; and at once set out with them to her brother's court where she was received with utmost joy.

In due time she returned to her husband with Sir Orson, who became emperor in his turn. But Sir Valentine succeeded King Pepin of France.

MADE AT THE
TEMPLE PRESS
LETCHWORTH

GREAT BRITAIN

A SELECTION OF THE
VOLUMES IN THE FICTION SECTION
OF THE

KINGS TREASURIES
OF LITERATURE

Suitable for Junior and Lower Middle Forms

KINGS TREASURIES OF LITERATURE

FICTION—*Contd.*

48pp. Prospectus post free.

J. M. DENT AND SONS LTD.
ALDINE HOUSE, BEDFORD ST., LONDON, W.C.2